A World of Fairy Tales

Published 1982 by
The Hamlyn Publishing Group Limited
London · New York · Sydney · Toronto
Astronaut House, Feltham, Middlesex, England
© Copyright The Hamlyn Publishing Group Limited 1982

ISBN 0 600 36496 8

Printed in Italy

A World of Fairy Tales

James Riordan

Hamlyn

London · New York · Sydney · Toronto

Contents

Introduction

This is a book of fairy tales, though few of the stories speak of fairies. Yet when children ask for a fairy story, these are just the sort of 'once upon a time' tales they have in mind. The line drawn between folk and fairy tale is wobbly and indistinct; but I have concentrated here not so much on the traditional folk tales which have been passed on from generation to generation by word of mouth, but rather on the beautifully-carved creations of writers like Hans Christian Andersen, Ibsen and Collodi, presented to an unseen audience.

In selecting tales, countries and mode of storytelling, I am guilty of bias. I have been guided by the wish to entertain and, most of all, to educate: to introduce children to cultures other than their own, to highlight morals of honesty, goodness and understanding, to give heroines an equal chance with heroes to excel.

Fairy tales have always attracted the best of the world's craftsmen: Tchaikovsky and Rimsky-Korsakov with their romantic music, Gustave Doré and Walter Crane with their imaginative art, Oscar Wilde and Leo Tolstoy with their enchanting writing.

Such is the enduring attraction of fairy tales. They are read over and over again, presented in comics and films, at a time when children are in the process of developing their own identity and expectations. They are read to children at their most impressionable age by teachers and parents, whom they trust above all others; and they are usually the first stories and films that children come into contact with. They are thus a part of education. Hence the importance of them being *good* literature: in words and deed.

We live in a remarkable age of television and space flights, tower blocks and instant foods; there are some today who curl a lip at the myths and legends of days gone by. The beloved tales of old may not be true, but they are not harmful or idle chatter; they have good reason for being in the world and for enduring. So, as the Irish poet W.B. Yeats once put it,

'Let us go forth, the tellers of tales, and seize whatever prey the heart long for, and have no fear. Everything exists, everything is true, and the earth is only a little dust under our feet.'

The Rainbow and the Bread Fruit Flower

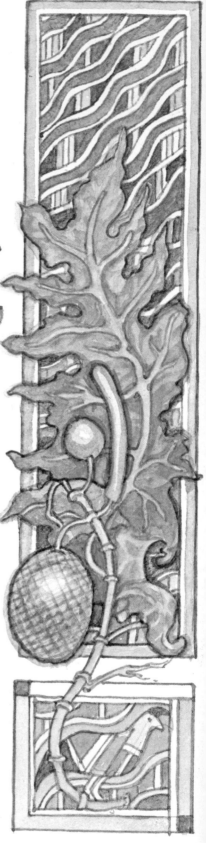

In the Dreamtime long ago in Australia, before the Moon was born, there lived three brothers on Peel Island. Their names were Walara, Nabijura and Kurramon. The elder brothers were strong and handsome; Kurramon was weak and plain.

In the passing of the days, a dark shadow fell upon the three young men; for they all fell in love with the selfsame girl, Lamari, and each wanted her for his wife.

Lamari lived alone in her mia-mia, making dillybags for folk to use. Her eyes were dark and shining and with her long fingers she could plait the strands of string into more dillybags than any other maid.

Walara and Nabijura decided to bring her food to win her love. 'Like that she will see we would make good husbands to provide for her,' they said. 'And we will make her choose between us.'

They agreed that the one she chose would not be envied by the other. First, Walara brought her fish fresh from the sea; but she refused to be his wife. Then Nabijura brought her game out of the bush; but she would not have him either.

It was then that Kurramon, the brother who was weak and plain, resolved to try his luck – even though his brothers sneered and called him names.

'Lamari won't choose you,' they said, and went off laughing.

Kurramon walked alone into the bush and gathered fruit to take to fair Lamari. Next he caught some fish and speared a kangaroo. Soon all the food he had gathered was more than that of his brothers.

But before taking his gift to the lovely maid, he decided to visit his mother's grave. It was full fourteen days since she had died. And as he pressed his hands upon the earth, his mother's strength passed into him and he felt big and strong.

Then boldly the youngest brother went with the food he'd gathered and asked Lamari to be his wife. She smiled, rose and took his hands in hers. For she loved him best.

And Lamari and Kurramon became man and wife.

Kurramon was now afraid that should his brothers learn about the pair they would do them harm. So he built a mia-mia in the bush and when he saw his brothers he did not speak of his wife, nor did he take her with him when he visited friends. But the brothers soon suspected something was amiss, for Lamari had disappeared.

One day, therefore, they followed Kurramon as he took food into the bush; they watched from behind a tree while he embraced his wife. What annoyed them most was the way she looked at him: for her eyes told them she loved him truly. Because of this they hated Kurramon and they debated the surest way to kill him.

When the three brothers next went hunting, the first two placed themselves so that Kurramon stood between them and the game they wished to spear. And as they threw their spears it was at him they aimed; yet he guessed their plan and swiftly dodged each hateful throw. He keenly watched their every move.

One day Walara and Nabijura invited Kurramon to go fishing with them on the reef. Though he knew they would likely try to drown him, he reluctantly agreed: for food was scarce and three could catch bigger fish than one.

Before he left with his brothers for the reef, he told Lamari of his fears, 'No doubt they will try to kill me and one will take you for his wife. If I die, a little bird will fly here with red drops of blood upon its beak; then you will know that I am dead.'

When she heard these words, all strength drained from Lamari and she could not speak. So Kurramon departed and went with his brothers to the fishing grounds. The two cruel brothers paddled the canoe to where they knew a giant clam lay on the reef; Kurramon knew nothing of it.

When they arrived, his brothers said, 'Dive down below the reef and spear some fish; meanwhile the two of us will hold the canoe against the wind.'

So Kurramon dived into the sea and swam down to the reef where the biggest fish were to be found. But as he searched the waters the giant clam suddenly seized both his hands and kept them trapped inside its shell. In several moments the waters of the sea moved into Kurramon's nose and mouth and he died upon the reef. His brothers, looking anxiously into the sea, saw the floating body still trapped by the giant clam, and they quickly paddled off in their canoe.

'Now we shall make Lamari choose between us,' said Walara. 'I'll go first since I'm the eldest; if she refuses me then you can court her.'

In the meantime, a little bird had flown to Lamari with red drops of blood upon its beak. And she knew what had been done.

Taking up her husband's spear she thrust it through her side, so hard it pinned her to the ground. In a moment she was dead.

Thus, when Walara reached Lamari's home, he found her dead. Afraid and angry, he quickly ran to Nabijura with the news.

'Let us go to the reef again,' he said, 'and fetch our

brother up. Perhaps we can bring him back to life and he can pull the spear out of his wife. That way she will live.'

Quickly Walara and Nabijura dragged their canoe into the sea and paddled fast to the reef where Kurramon had died. They searched the waters until at last they saw his body drifting lightly with the waves; then it was gone.

In the stillness that followed the brothers held their breath, scanning the waters for a sign. Suddenly, a fish of many colours sped up from the reef, broke through the water and flew up in an arc into the sky, moving with the speed of a driven spear. It curved back to the sea far away, leaving a trail of colour that men call the Rainbow.

Walara and Nabijura went back sadly to the beach and the Rainbow followed; it spread its arc across the bush until it reached the mia-mia where Lamari lay. And when it touched her lifeless form, the colours enclosed her so that she became the Bread Fruit Flower that grows beneath the Rainbow.

And now, when the Sun and rain visit the world together, the Bread Fruit blooms and the Rainbow stands guard over it.

Thus will it be forever.

The Twelve Months

In a little village in the mountains of Bohemia, there once lived an old woman with her daughter and stepdaughter, Jana. The woman doted on her own child but little Jana could do nothing to please her.

While the lazy daughter lay all day on a feather bed eating honey cakes, Jana would fetch firewood from the forest, draw water from the well, scrub the washing in the cold mountain stream and water the flower-beds. How well she knew the winter frost and summer Sun, the soft spring breeze and autumn rain.

That may be why she met all twelve months of the year together.

It happened one winter, well into the month of January. So thickly had the snow fallen that paths had to be cleared before folk could leave their cottages. On the wooded mountain slopes, the firs and pines stood waist-deep in snow, unable to sway when the wind whistled through their frosty boughs. The villagers stayed indoors and stoked up their stoves.

14

It was during that time, one cold evening, that the cruel stepmother unlatched the cottage door and peered into the raging blizzard; turning back, she told her stepdaughter, 'Go to the forest and pick some snowdrops. It is your sister's birthday tomorrow.'

Jana stared in disbelief: would her stepmother really send her out into the forest? It was so dark and cold out there. And what snowdrops would she find in the depths of winter? They never appeared from their earthy beds till March.

Her sister added spitefully, 'Even if you do get lost, no one will shed tears for you. Here, take this basket and don't come back until it's full.'

Tears filled Jana's eyes as she pulled a ragged scarf about her shoulders and went out into the driving snow. The wind powdered her eyes with snowflakes and tore at her threadbare coat. Yet she stumbled on, barely able to drag each footstep free of the clinging snow.

Night drew its dark veil more tightly about her, leaving

but the dull whiteness beneath her feet. Presently she arrived at the very edge of the forest; it was so black there that she could not see her hand before her face. Chilled and frightened, she sank down on a fallen tree to await her fate.

Then, all of a sudden, she spied a light flickering some way off amid the trees – like a fallen star entangled in the branches. At first she thought she had imagined it, then she rose and walked towards the glow, making her way slowly through the snowdrifts and the frost-covered bracken.

'If only it will stay alight,' she prayed.

And it did. The nearer she came, the brighter it glowed. But it was no star: now she could smell warm smoke and hear the crackle of burning brushwood.

Before she realized it, she found herself in a clearing bathed in light. In the centre, a blazing bonfire spiralled fierce and tall towards the sky. And round the fire sat men quietly talking, some close to the flames, some farther off.

Jana wondered who they all could be. They were certainly not like hunters or woodmen – they were dressed too handsomely for that: some in silver, some in gold, and some in green and yellow velvet.

Looking round the group, she saw that there were three old men, three of middle years, three youths and three just boys still. Twelve in all.

The Twelve Months!

Just at that instant, one old man, the tallest, with the longest beard and bushiest eyebrows, turned and stared directly at her. Jana was so afraid, she wanted to run away. But it was too late.

The old man hailed her in a booming voice, 'Whence comest thou? What brings thee here?'

Jana showed her empty basket. 'I have to pick a basketful of snowdrops,' she said.

The old man's laughter rang throughout the forest. 'Snowdrops in January? Art thou dreaming, maid?'

'My stepmother sent me here for snowdrops,' said Jana quietly, 'and forbade me to return without them.'

At that, all Twelve Months turned towards her, then murmured low amongst themselves.

Though Jana listened hard, she could not catch their words or understand their tongue; it was like the trees rustling and the wind whistling. At last the glade was silent.

Then the tall elder again addressed her, 'What, pray,

wilt thou do if thou hast no snowdrops?'

'I shall stay in the forest,' she replied, 'and await the month of March. I would rather freeze here than return without them.' And she began to cry.

One of the twelve, the youngest and merriest, stood up and approached the tall old man. 'Brother January, I beseech thee, let me take thy place for a single hour.'

Stroking his long beard thoughtfully, the old man answered, 'Gladly would I grant thee an hour, Brother, but March cannot come before the month of February.'

'Let February come, too,' spoke up another elder, this one a shaggy-browed greybeard. 'Then March may take an hour, I mind not. We all know the maid anyway: we meet her at the ice-hole with her pails, or on the woodland path with her bundle of sticks. She's a maid for all seasons, right enough. We must do what we can to help her.'

'So be it,' said January, striking the ground with his icy staff and chanting to the wind,

'Frost, O Frost, cold master of the ice,
Pray melt thy frozen heart;
Untie thy stiff bonds in a trice
And let the snowdrifts part.
Sturdy fir and lofty pine,
Shake free your crystal lace;
Frozen snows, at once recline,
January yields his place.'

As the old man finished, a hush descended upon the forest: the ice-covered trees ceased to creak, and soft snow began to fall thickly in large flakes.

'Now it is thy turn, Brother,' said January handing the staff to February.

He too struck the ground with the icy staff and cried,

'Wind, tempest, storm and gale,
Blow with all your might.
Blizzard, furies, sleet and hail,
Rage into the night.
Plough your furrows through the snow,
Sweep across the lake.
Drive the ground wind high and low,
Twisting like a snake.'

No sooner had he finished than a bleak wind began to lash the branches, scudding snowflakes whirled about and white whirlwinds danced across the ground.

February passed the icy staff to his younger brother, saying, 'Now it is up to thee, Brother March.'

Merry March seized the staff and struck the ground. As

Jana gazed in wonder, she saw the staff was no longer made of ice: it was now a sturdy bud-filled branch.

March chuckled happily and burst into song,

'Babble gaily, melting brook,
Ripple, glistening pool;
Ants awake and leave your nook,
Gone the winter cruel.
Birds return and sing your song,
Disperse the forest gloom.
Bears and squirrels, come along,
And tender snowdrops bloom.'

Jana threw up her hands in amazement: where had all the snowdrifts gone? Where were the icicles that had hung from every bough? Beneath her feet stretched a carpet of brown earth, clear of snow. All about her life was stirring, flowering, buzzing. Buds were sprouting on the branches and the first green shoots peeped out from under their covers.

'Make haste,' commanded March. 'My brothers have granted us a single hour together.'

Jana quickly ran to gather snowdrops. The ground was thick with them: under bushes and stones, on mounds and hillocks and grassy knolls, as far as she could see. She picked a whole basketful, then hurried back to the glade where the fire had burned and the Twelve Brothers sat.

But the fire was gone . . . And the brothers too.

It was still light in the clearing, yet not as before: the light came from the full Moon that had risen.

Dismayed that there was nobody to thank, Jana ran home with her basket of flowers. Her feet seemed to glide over the mossy soil as she made her way back to the wooden cottage. However, no sooner had she entered than the

winter blizzard again rattled the shutters and the Moon
vanished behind the black storm clouds.

'Why are you back so soon?' cried her stepmother and
sister together. 'Where are the snowdrops?'

Jana said nothing. Lifting up her basket, she tipped the
snowdrops on to the table.

The stepmother and her daughter could scarcely believe
their eyes. 'Wherever did you find them?' they gasped.

Jana told her story. They listened dumbly, nodding and
shaking their heads in turn. There were the snowdrops on
the table, a whole heap of them – sweet, frail snowdrops
that brought the fresh fragrance of spring into the room.

'What else did the Twelve Months give you?' asked the
stepmother.

'I asked for nothing more,' Jana replied.

'How stupid you are!' exclaimed her sister. 'Folk seldom
see all Twelve Months together. And all you asked for was
snowdrops! I would have demanded juicy apples and pears

from October, strawberries from July, white mushrooms from September, fresh cucumbers from May . . .'

'Clever girl, daughter,' said her mother. 'In winter, strawberries and pears are worth their weight in gold. And that little fool fetched snowdrops! Wrap yourself up warmly, my dear, and hurry to that glade. They won't cheat you with a basket of silly flowers.'

'I should say not!' snorted her daughter, thrusting her arms into a fur coat and tying a warm scarf about her head.

She left the cottage and hurried along, following her sister's footprints as best she could. The forest was dark, the night chill, the clouds grey; the snowdrifts seemed to grow higher, towering over her on all sides.

'Oh dear,' she groaned, 'why did I have to come out on a night like this? I should be lying at home in my warm bed instead of freezing in the snow. I shall surely lose my way.'

Hardly had the thought entered her head than she glimpsed a light far off, among the trees.

She made for the light, ploughing her way through the snow until she came to a clearing. In the centre blazed a huge bonfire and round it sat twelve men, talking quietly.

The daughter went straight up to the fire, making no curtsy, nor uttering a word of greeting. She just made room for herself by the fireside and began to warm her frozen hands and feet.

The Twelve Months fell silent.

By and by, the month of January struck the ground with his staff. 'Who art thou?' he asked.

'Just now my sister was here,' the girl replied. 'I followed her footprints in the snow. You gave her a basketful of snowdrops.'

'We know thy sister well,' said January, 'but we have never set eyes on thee before. What is thy business with us?'

'I am here for my gifts,' the girl said boldly. 'I want strawberries from July, the very biggest he can find. From August I want big hazel nuts; from September white mushrooms; from October . . .'

'Not so fast,' interrupted January. 'Summer never comes before spring, nor spring before winter. July is still a long way off. It is I who presently rule the seasons and I shall reign for my full one and thirty days.'

'My, my, what a gruff old man you are!' said the daughter. 'Anyway, I didn't come for you. You are good for nothing but snow and frost. I want the summer months.'

January scowled. 'Then seek summer in winter!' he roared.

With a wave of his broad sleeves, he raised such a furious snowstorm in the forest that the entire glade was soon enveloped in swirling, blinding snow. It even blotted out the fire's light. The girl could only hear the angry snapping, fizzing and hissing of the flames.

She became very frightened. 'Stop it,' she cried. 'Where are you?'

The snowstorm snatched at her, blinding her eyes and taking her breath away. She rushed about in panic, fell headlong into a snowdrift and was quickly swallowed up in the snow.

In the meantime, her mother was waiting impatiently at the cottage door, peering through the blizzard for a sign of her daughter's return. Finally, she could wait no longer: wrapping herself up in her warmest clothes, she hastened off into the forest.

She plunged deeper and deeper into the snow, shouting and cursing, until she too was swallowed by the storm.

Jana, however, lived on contentedly and peaceably in the cottage, grew up, wed and raised a family. And round her cottage, so folk say, there appeared the most wonderful garden; in it roses bloomed, berries ripened, apples and pears grew in abundance the whole year round.

'That Mistress has all Twelve Months visiting her at once,' folk would say.

And they were certainly correct.

The Black Bull of Norroway

Long ago in Scotland, there lived in Norroway a widow with three daughters. And they were very poor with scarce enough to bind a body to a soul.

When the eldest lass had come of age, she told her mother, 'Mother, bake me a bannock and roast me a collop. I'm away to seek my fortune.'

Her mother did so, and the daughter went to an old washerwife living in the dell, to seek her fortune: for the wife was said to be fair canny.

'Good day to you, washerwife,' she said in greeting at the cottage door.

'Good day t'ye, ma bonny lass,' the washerwife replied. 'What will ye be wanting of me?'

'I wish to know my fortune, Ma'am,' she said; and curtseyed low besides.

The washerwife made her welcome: 'Bide aweel, ma bonny lass, and ye'll see your fortune soon enough. Go down the passage, unlatch the kitchen door and ye'll see what is to be.'

So the eldest daughter went down the passage, opened the kitchen door and peered outside. She saw naught the first day or the next; but on the third she looked again and saw a coach and six white horses coming down the road. At once she ran in to the washerwife and told her all she'd seen.

'Ye've seen your fortune,' the woman said, 'yon's for you.'

So the daughter rode away in the coach-and-six.

By and by, the second daughter came of age and told her mother, 'Mother, bake me a bannock and roast me a collop. I'm away to seek my fortune.'

Her mother did so, and away she went to the old washerwife in the dell, just as her sister had. And the same tale unfolded as before. She saw naught the first day or the next; but on the third she looked again and saw a coach with four black horses coming down the road.

'Yon's for you,' the washerwife said.

So the second daughter rode away in the coach-and-four.

Meanwhile, in the widow's home, the youngest daughter came of age and told her mother, 'Mother, bake me a bannock and roast me a collop. I'm away to seek my fortune.'

Her mother did so, and off the daughter went to the washerwife in the dell.

'Ye'll see your fortune down the passage and through the kitchen door,' the washerwife said. 'There ye'll see what is to be.'

The lassie saw naught the first day or the next. But on the third she looked and looked again. For there, coming down the road, was a big Black Bull, blowing and bellowing for all he could.

Hastily she shut the door and told the washerwife what she'd seen.

'Aweel,' the woman said, 'ye've seen your fortune. Yon Black Bull has come for you.'

Aye she wept, and loud she wept. But what is to be will be. Up on to the Bull's broad back she climbed, sobbing, and off they went.

Aye they travelled, and on they travelled, till the lass grew faint with hunger. It was then the Black Bull spoke.

'Eat from my right ear,
Drink from my left,
And you will be refreshed.'

She did as she was told and felt refreshed.

Long they rode, and hard they rode, till they came in sight of a braw big castle.

'That's where we will spend the night,' the Bull declared. 'My eldest brother is laird within.'

Presently they reached the castle. Servants hastened to lift her off the Bull's broad back, take her in and send the Bull to a field to graze. How surprised the lassie was to find her eldest sister living there with the castle laird. They talked long into the night; then maid-servants took her to a rich bed-chamber, bathed and undressed her, wrapped

her in a soft silk sleeping robe and tucked her up in bed. So weary was she, and so snug, that she fell asleep at once and slept soundly till the dawn.

Next morning, she was bathed and dressed once more, then given a rosy apple.

'Keep this apple whole,' her sister said, 'until you are in direst need. Then it will help you.'

Thereupon she was taken out and set upon the Black Bull's back. And off they went once more.

Far they journeyed, farther aye than I can tell, till the lass was faint with hunger. Once again the Black Bull guessed her thoughts, and kindly said,

'Eat from my right ear,
Drink from my left,
And you will be refreshed.'

She did as he said and felt refreshed, then fell asleep. When she awoke she saw yonder a braw big castle, even bonnier than the first.

'That's where we will stay the night,' the Black Bull said. 'My second brother is laird within.'

Soon they reached the castle. How glad the lassie was to find her second sister waiting at the gate. Servants came to help her down, take her in and send the Bull away into a field to graze. The evening passed in happy chatter with her sister; the night passed as comfortably as the one before. Then in the morning she was given a golden pear.

'Keep this pear whole,' her sister said, 'until you are in dire need; then it will help you.'

Again she was set upon the Black Bull's back, and off they went. Long they rode, aye hard they rode, until they came to a braw big castle, the bonniest she'd ever seen.

'That's where we will spend the night,' the Black Bull said. 'It is my home.'

Directly they arrived, servants came to lift her down, take her in and send the Bull to graze. In the morning she was given a purple plum.

'Keep this plum whole,' the Black Bull said, 'till you are in great need; then it will help you.'

After that she was set upon the Black Bull's back, and off they went again.

And aye they rode, and on they rode, till the lass felt faint with hunger. And right away the Bull spoke up,

'Eat from my right ear,
Drink from my left,
And you will be refreshed.'

She did as he said and felt refreshed, then fell asleep.
When she awoke she found herself in the mouth of a dark
and gloomy glen. And to her surprise the Bull was a bull no
more: a handsome stranger stood before her. He told her
that he was indeed a prince. But a wicked witch had cast a
spell upon him which would last full seven years. Till then
he had to take his Black Bull form.

In an instant he became the Bull again.

'Fair lassie,' said the Bull to her, 'seat yourself on yonder
stone, and keep ye still as still; move not hand nor foot till I
return. I must away to battle with the Etin. Now mind thee
well: if all about ye turns to blue, ye'll ken that I have won.
If all about ye turns to red, ye'll ken that I am dead.'

As the Black Bull vanished through the glen, the lassie
sat herself down upon the stone to wait and hope. For she
loved the handsome prince and did not wish to see him die.

So she sat there in the murky gloom, black shadows
enfolding her slender form, the wind hissing and spitting in
the trees. By and by – it seemed an age – the wind ceased to
hiss, the shadows faded and all about her turned to blue.

Overjoyed, the lassie stamped her foot and clapped her
hands, so happy was she that the Bull was saved. Alas, by
moving hand and foot, she had broken the solemn vow.
Thus it was, when the Bull returned, he could not find her,
nor she him: for they were now invisible one to the other.

Long she sat, and aye she sat, till she was tired of waiting.
At last she rose and went away; she knew not where to seek
him. On and on she wandered, past loch and burn, until
she came to a mountain of crystal glass. Every time she
went to climb, she slipped back down again. So finally she
gave up, and walked sadly along a foothill path. All at once
she found herself before a blacksmith's forge, where an old
man plied the bellows.

The smith promised, if she would serve him seven years,
he'd make her a pair of iron shoes; with these she could
climb Glass Mountain. And serve him she did full seven
years.

When her time was up she put on the iron shoes and
climbed the mountain with ease. As she came down the
other side, she saw a white-washed cottage in the distance.

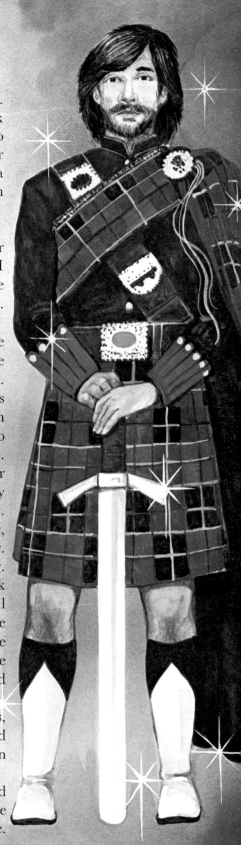

27

Outside the cottage was an old witch washerwife, bending over a wash tub and scrubbing a blood-stained shirt. Going up to the woman, the lassie asked if she might stay the night.

'If ye can wash the blood-stains from this shirt, ye can bide aweel,' the old hag muttered. 'The shirt belongs to the Prince of Norroway who is lying sick within after long years of battle; he bloodied his shirt fighting with the Etin. But not I, nor my daughter can wash the stains away. The more we scrub, the darker are the stains.'

At that the stranger lassie set to work, and as soon as she began, the stains came out, the shirt was pure and clean.

The witch washerwife cackled and rubbed her hands in glee. For, truth to tell, the Prince was bound to wed whoever washed his stained shirt clean. And now the witch hurried to him with the shirt, telling him her daughter had washed it.

So the news was spread that the Prince and the ugly washerwife's daughter were to wed the very next day. The young stranger lassie's eyes filled with tears when she heard the tidings, for she guessed that the Prince was her lost love.

What could she do?

It was then that she recalled her rosy apple. Right away she took it out and, breaking it in two, she found it full of grains of gold – the richest ever seen. At once she showed them to the witch's daughter.

'All these are yours,' she said, 'if you put off your wedding for just one day and let me go to the Prince's room tonight.'

The greedy girl agreed. 'Very well, let it be. Tonight, when he's asleep, you may enter his room.'

Night came. The lassie went to the Prince's room and found him fast asleep. He could not be wakened, for the canny witch had given him a sleeping draught. All night long the poor lass wept and sang beside his bed:

'Seven long years I served for thee,
The Mountain of Glass I climbed for thee,
The blood-stained shirt I washed for thee,
Wilt thou not waken and speak to me?'

But the Prince did not hear her and, at dawn, she had to leave.

What could she do now?

Then she recalled the golden pear. Straightaway she took it out and, breaking it in two, she found it full of pearls – the richest ever seen. With these she bargained with the bride-to-be to put off her wedding just another day so that she might spend a night in the Prince's room. It was agreed.

As night fell, the lassie entered his room and saw him lying, pale and handsome, in deepest slumber. Long she sat, and aye she sang throughout the night:

'Seven long years I served for thee,
The Mountain of Glass I climbed for thee,
The blood-stained shirt I washed for thee,
Wilt thou not waken and speak to me?'

But the Prince slept on soundly, for the evil washerwife had given him another sleeping draught. And at dawn's first light she had to leave.

What could she do now?

The purple plum was her last hope. Breaking it open, she found it full of blood-red rubies – the richest ever seen. With these she made one last bargain with the bride-to-be and went that night with heavy heart into the Prince's room.

Long she sat, and aye she sang her song:

'Seven long years I served for thee,
The Mountain of Glass I climbed for thee,
The blood-stained shirt I washed for thee,
Wilt thou not waken and speak to me?'

All in vain. The poor lass was in despair: again and again she tried to rouse him. And when it was almost light she stroked his dark hair as she wept her last farewell. A hot tear rolled down her cheek and fell upon the Prince's shoulder, burning him. At last he stirred and opened his eyes. Seeing the bonny lassie, he took her in his arms.

She told him all that had befallen her. And he told her all that had befallen him. Now all was well. The old witch washerwife and her ugly daughter were banished from the land. The Prince of Norroway and the bonny lassie returned to the Prince's braw castle and were wed.

And he and she are living happy to this day, for aught I ken.

The Blue Baba of the Marsh

In the village of Polevaya in Russia's Ural Mountains, there lived a lad named Yuri. He was all alone in the world, having buried the last of his family. But each had left him something: from his father he'd broad hands and shoulders, from his mother a bold tongue, and from Granny Fedosya . . . well, let me tell you of that.

Before Granny Fedosya died, she called Yuri to her and said, 'Listen, my lad, take the three feathers in my sieve and they will serve you well – the white one is for bright day to cheer you, the black is for night to guard you, the red is for the Sun to bring you joy. Now, don't go chasing after gold; it comes in grains and goes in dust. The only lasting treasure you'll ever get is from the Blue Baba of the Marsh and that only when she changes to a pretty maid and gives it with her own fair hands. She rewards none but those with quick wits, firm will and a kind heart. None other.'

When she died, Yuri took the feathers from her sieve and

tied them with blue thread to his fur cap. In that way, he thought, he would always remember Granny Fedosya's words and they would bring him luck.

One day soon after, Yuri returned to his work in the goldfield over by Serpent Hill. It was a fine day so on his way he took a short cut across the marsh. The spring sun was warm and he hoped it had dried the ground enough for him to pick his way.

At first he jogged easily through the crisp bracken, but soon he found his feet clinging to the quaggy soil. It was hard to keep a straight path, hopping from tuft to tuft. He wanted to go one way, but the tufts led him another. At last he found himself in a glade carpeted by feathergrass and clover, with clusters of marsh marigolds and clumps of bog oak. The ground here was dry and firm. Though thankful for a rest, Yuri feared he was lost; he had crossed the marsh more times than he could recall, but he had never set eyes on this glade before.

He made his way through the clearing and down a slope to a little round pool. Although he could not see the bottom, the water was crystal clear, like a woodland spring. A bluish web spanned the pool, and in the centre squatted a fat blue spider.

Yuri was thirsty, so he brushed the web aside to take a drink. As he did that he became so dizzy he almost toppled over.

'Phew, this marsh has made me tired,' he said to himself. 'I'd best take a rest for an hour or so.'

He struggled to get up, but found he had barely enough strength to crawl up the slope. Just then something happened that all but made his eyes pop out. A little old woman was rising from the pool. She was no taller than his knee. Her tiny dress was blue, her headscarf was blue, and she was bluish blue herself; and such a scraggy figure that a puff of wind would surely blow her away. Yet her blue eyes were young and so big they seemed not to belong to her face at all.

The little old woman stared at the lad and stretched out her arms towards him. And the arms just grew and grew. Soon they were almost touching his head. Her hands were slender, like wisps of blue mist, with no apparent strength in them; nor were they tipped by claws, yet they were terrifying all the same. Yuri wished he could crawl away, but he could not move.

He tried to turn his head so that he might escape the great, blue, staring eyes. As he strained hard, the feathers in his cap tickled his nose and made him sneeze. He sneezed and sneezed until his nose bled, and still he could not stop. But the sneezing seemed to clear his head. He scooped up his cap and scrambled to his feet, away from the scrawny hag.

He gave his nose a good hard blow and said with a grin, 'Too bad, old woman, I'm too clever for you.'

He spat on his hands and turned to go. But she called after him in a voice as clear and tuneful as a maid's, 'Don't crow too soon, my lad. Next time I'll have the head from off your shoulders.'

'No fear of that,' retorted Yuri. 'I won't be coming back again.'

'Ah, you're scared, you're scared of a little old woman,' she babbled gaily.

The taunt stung Yuri. He halted at the edge of the grassy glade. 'If I were to return,' he called back, 'I'd come to spite you and I would draw water from your pool.'

At that the little old woman hooted with laughter and began to tease him. 'It's only thanks to Granny Fedosya that you escaped me. Her feathers won't help you next time; my hands will drag you down to the bottom. There's not a man alive can drink water from my pool.'

'We'll see about that,' replied Yuri boldly. 'I'll be back on Sunday.' And he made his way out of the marsh, marking the path carefully.

'So that's what she's like,' he said to himself, 'the Blue Baba of the Marsh. A real witch with the eyes of a young maid and a voice as clear as crystal. I'd certainly like to see her change into a fair young girl.'

Yuri had heard much about the Blue Baba. Many's the tale they told of her in the goldfields. Folk might see her in old mines or marshes. A fortune was said to lie beneath her; and the person who could shift her would claim a gleaming hoard of gold and precious stones. Many were said to have tried, but they had either returned empty-handed or not come back at all.

It was dusk before Yuri arrived at the goldfield. He said nothing of his adventures. Instead he pretended he had been seeing to his grandmother's affairs and he showed the three feathers that she had given him: white for the day, black for the night, and red for the Sun.

Now one of the goldpanners, Kuzma, made up his mind to steal the feathers for himself, thinking they would bring good luck. That night, when everyone was asleep, Kuzma took them from the fur cap. Yuri was upset to find them gone, and thought he must have dropped them somewhere, but next Sunday, he woke early and prepared for his trip into the marsh. The loss of his feathers wasn't going to stop him! He took along a pan with a long pole fastened to it, with which to scoop up water from the pool.

All that week, Kuzma had kept an eye on Yuri, sure he was keeping some secret to himself. Now he followed close behind, clutching the three feathers tightly.

It took Yuri some time to trace his marks back to the glade, but when he arrived at the pool, there was the little old woman waiting for him.

'So, the cock sparrow's back again, is he?' she trilled gaily. 'And he's lost his Granny's feathers by the look of things. What'll he do now, I wonder?'

She stood a little to one side, and did not reach out for him this time. There was a thick mist hanging over the pool like a pale sapphire crown. Yuri took a run down the slope, swung the long handle of his pan towards the middle of the crown and dipped it into the pool.

'Mind I don't smack you on the nose with my pan, old witch,' he shouted.

Yuri scooped up a panful of water, but found it so heavy he could hardly lift the pole. The little old crone laughed, showing her young white teeth.

'Come on, come on,' she mocked, 'just try to pull your pan out. Let's see how much water you can drink!'

He put all his strength into the next effort, managed to raise the pan a little and struggled to tip it over the old woman. But the pole snapped and spilled all the water back into the pool. That really set her off, hands on hips, rocking backwards and forwards, giggling like a silly maid.

'You wait, old hag, I'll souse you yet,' Yuri muttered.

Then the old woman grew serious and said, 'Well, that's enough, we've had our fun. I can see you're a brave fellow. So mark this: come when the Moon is full and I'll show you treasures of every sort. You can take all that you can carry.'

'The only treasure I want is to see you as a young maid,' said Yuri.

'Well now, we'll see about that,' laughed the old woman, flashing her young blue eyes and white teeth.

In the meantime, of course, Kuzma was watching all and listening from behind a tree. 'I must get back to the goldfield before Yuri,' he muttered. 'I'll prepare some sacks to carry off the treasure.'

Kuzma hurried off. But Yuri made his way across the marsh, until he arrived back safely at his Granny's hut. That evening he was surprised to discover that Granny Fedosya's sieve was gone; he wondered who could have taken it, for it was quite worthless.

Several days passed, yet he could not get the Blue Baba from his mind. At night, he dreamed and by day he mused as he worked – those deep blue eyes haunted him, the flute-like voice disturbed his thoughts. 'Come when the Moon is full,' she'd said so softly and so sweetly, it touched his heart.

At last he made up his mind that he would go back, saying to himself, 'At least I'll see what kind of treasure it is and, who knows, she might even show herself as a young maid.'

With summer approaching, the nights were getting lighter and the Moon fuller. One day, word went round the goldfield that Kuzma had disappeared. A search-party was sent out, but no one found any trace of him. The bailiff was far from pleased, since he'd to answer to the Tsar for missing workers on the crownlands. But nothing could be done. Kuzma was gone, and that was that.

Yuri set off on a night when the Moon was high. In no time at all he reached the glade, yet found it empty. Still, he was cautious and did not descend the slope at once. He just whispered softly, 'I've come to take the treasure from your own fair hands.'

No sooner had he uttered these words than the little old woman appeared and said, 'You are most welcome, dear guest. I've waited long. Come, take all you can carry.'

She passed her hands above the pool as if raising a lid, and in the twinkling of an eye, there it was, filled to the brim with all kinds of precious stones. Yuri longed to touch the treasure, but he would not move closer.

The old crone tried to coax him. 'Come on now, why stand there like a stubborn mule? Come and take as much as your sack will hold.'

'I have no sack,' Yuri replied. 'And Granny Fedosya told me differently. There's only one lasting treasure, she said; and that you give a man yourself.'

'Well I never, there's no pleasing the young master,' said

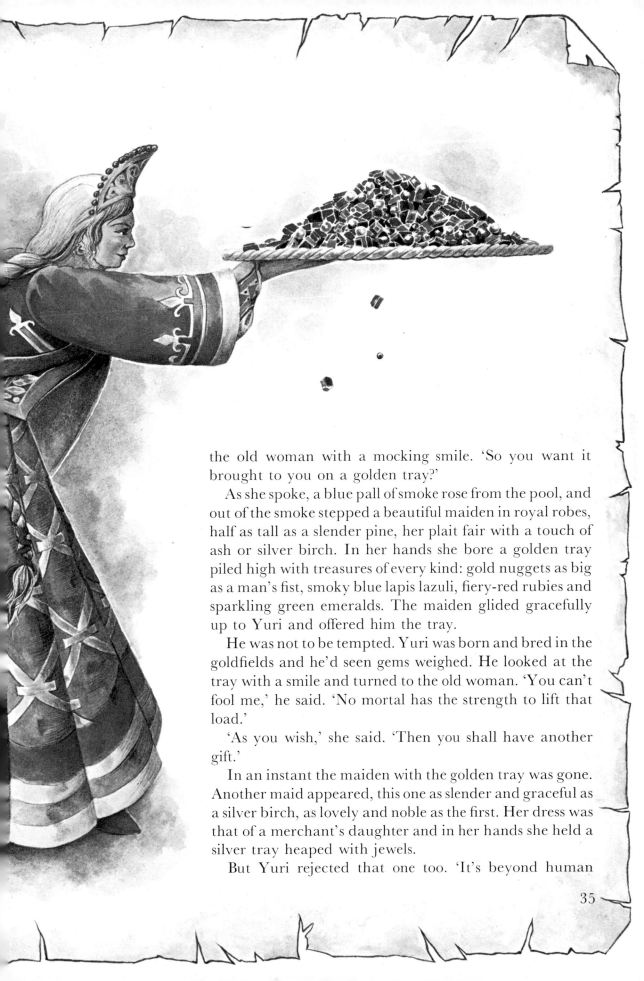

the old woman with a mocking smile. 'So you want it brought to you on a golden tray?'

As she spoke, a blue pall of smoke rose from the pool, and out of the smoke stepped a beautiful maiden in royal robes, half as tall as a slender pine, her plait fair with a touch of ash or silver birch. In her hands she bore a golden tray piled high with treasures of every kind: gold nuggets as big as a man's fist, smoky blue lapis lazuli, fiery-red rubies and sparkling green emeralds. The maiden glided gracefully up to Yuri and offered him the tray.

He was not to be tempted. Yuri was born and bred in the goldfields and he'd seen gems weighed. He looked at the tray with a smile and turned to the old woman. 'You can't fool me,' he said. 'No mortal has the strength to lift that load.'

'As you wish,' she said. 'Then you shall have another gift.'

In an instant the maiden with the golden tray was gone. Another maid appeared, this one as slender and graceful as a silver birch, as lovely and noble as the first. Her dress was that of a merchant's daughter and in her hands she held a silver tray heaped with jewels.

But Yuri rejected that one too. 'It's beyond human

strength to lift it,' he explained. 'And besides, you're not giving it to me yourself.'

At that the old crone laughed a merry tinkling laugh that danced around the glade. 'All right, have it your own way,' she said. 'I'll please you and myself as well. But mind you don't regret it afterwards. Just wait here awhile.'

Both she and the maid with the silver tray were gone in a swirl of mist. Yuri waited patiently, but no one came. He was about to turn for home when the trees rustled behind him. He turned towards the sound and saw a young girl approaching, a mortal girl of human height. Her robe was blue, her headscarf blue, and she wore blue slippers on her feet. And oh, how pretty she was! Her eyes twinkled like sapphires, her pale skin was gently brushed by woodland dew, her lips were full and red like wild strawberries, and her russet plait was tossed forward over one slender shoulder and tied with a scarlet ribbon.

She came right up to Yuri and softly said, 'Please accept this gift, dear Yuri, from a heart that is young and pure.'

She offered him Granny Fedosya's sieve filled with forest berries. There were wild strawberries and raspberries, golden cloudberries, bilberries and cranberries – all the fruits of the forest. The sieve was piled high with them. On top lay three feathers: one white, one black and one red, tied together with blue thread.

In silence, Yuri took the sieve of berries, but stood there as one lost. Where had she come from? How had she picked all those berries at that time of year? Who was she?

The girl gave a gentle laugh, and said, 'Folk call me Blue Baba of the Marsh. But to those with quick wits, firm will and a kind heart, I show myself as you see me now.'

She told him of Kuzma, how he had come for the treasure, but had plunged into the pool, dragging his sacks to the bottom with him. 'Only these three feathers of yours floated to the top. It is plain you have a kind and pure heart,' she said.

Yuri did not know what to say. She, too, stood there in silence, shyly toying with the scarlet ribbon in her hair.

At last she spoke again, 'So there it is, dear Yuri. I am the Blue Baba. Ever old, ever young, set here to guard the pool's treasures for all time.'

She again fell silent, then said quietly, 'Well, that will do. Come now, or you'll be seeing me forever in your dreams.'

She sighed so deeply, it was like a knife piercing Yuri's heart. If only, he thought, she could remain a mortal maid, a girl he might wed and love for all his life. But it was not to be. In a swirl of purple haze she was gone for good.

For a long while Yuri stood as if rooted to the ground, just like the marsh oaks in the wood. A damp blue mist from the pool slowly crept through the glade, and only then did he turn for home, clutching his sieve of berries. It was almost dawn when he arrived.

As he entered his hut, a strange thing happened. The sieve suddenly grew very heavy and the bottom burst, scattering precious stones upon the wooden floor.

With such a fine fortune, Yuri bought his freedom straightaway. He lived well enough to the end of his days but, though girls from far and near sought his company, he could never bring himself to wed. For he could not forget the blue maid of the forest pool.

Fairies of the Evening Star

Many snows in the past there was no winter with its cold blasts and piercing chill, and men and beasts lived in peace and contentment. There was food in plenty for everyone, for many deer roamed the forests around the Great Lakes, herds of buffalo grazed on the prairies of the west and fish abounded in the streams that flow from the mountains towards the rising Sun. Flowers blossomed everywhere and the birds, clad in brighter plumage than today, filled the air with happy song.

There was no war.

There was no fear between men, since no one had cause to harm another.

One time in this long-ago land, there was an Indian chief who had ten daughters, all as lovely as the Moon. When they grew to be women, nine daughters married young Indian braves. But the youngest would not listen to the handsome braves who came to woo her; she told them simply, 'I am happy as I am.'

And yet, in the course of time, she married an old, old man, with snow-white hair and bandy legs. This made her father and sisters angry, but she just smiled and told them simply, 'I am happy as I am.'

One day, the father held a party for his daughters and their husbands. And on the way to their father's lodge the sisters taunted the youngest maid, 'Poor girl, what a pity she married that ugly old man. See, he can hardly walk; were he to stumble he would surely be unable to get up.'

As they walked along they noticed the old man glancing up at the Evening Star and, every now and then, uttering a soft low call.

'See now,' a sister laughed, 'the old fool thinks the Star's his father and will protect him.'

And they all laughed in scorn.

Presently, they passed a hollow log about as wide as a boy or girl. How surprised they were to see the old man fall to his hands and knees and crawl in at one end. But when he emerged at the other, lo and behold, he was no longer an aged man; he was tall and handsome, a proud young Indian brave. His wife, however, was no longer a youthful maid; she was now a bent old woman hobbling with a stick.

As the sisters walked on in wonder, they saw the handsome brave take good care of his aged wife, helping her gently along the way. He seemed to love her more dearly than before.

The ten wives and their men came to the father's lodge and began the meal. All was forgotten in the merry feasting until a voice spoke to the handsome brave. It seemed to come down from the skies. Glancing up they saw the Evening Star shining through the smoke hole of the lodge.

'My son,' the Star began. 'Many moons ago, as you well know, an evil spirit changed you into a bent old man. That spirit has lost its power now because of the sacrifice of your wife and you are free. You may come home to live with me and bring all your relatives as well; your wife shall regain her youth and you shall both have all that you desire.'

All at once, the lodge rose into the air. As it floated

upwards the wooden bark changed to the gossamer wings of a million tiny insects. And as the young chief gazed upon his wife he saw that she was a lovely squaw once more. Her buckskin dress was now of shining satin, and her wooden stick became a silver feather in her hair. But the scornful father, sisters and their menfolk had turned into brightly-coloured birds: some were jays and some were parrots, some were orioles and some parakeets. And all sang most divinely.

Up, up sailed the lodge until it reached the Evening Star where all was silvery white and peaceful. How happy the Star was to see his son.

As the birds flew joyfully about the Star, the son sat down at his father's feet with his young squaw by his side. The father welcomed them into his home and gave them all they wanted. They lived happily together for several years and in time a son was born.

As the boy grew up he yearned to hunt and shoot with bows and arrows. Since the Evening Star loved his little grandson he taught him all the skills of hunting; but he gave a solemn warning, 'On no account should you shoot a bird; woe betide you if you do.'

For many days the little brave shot his arrows into the air, at trees and shrubs and blades of silver grass. But he soon tired of this sport and longed to fire at a moving bird. So when no one was looking he aimed his arrows at the birds; they were much harder to hit than a standing tree. One day, however, he crept up behind an oriole and caught it unawares. He let loose an arrow that flew straight and true, and sank deep into the oriole's breast. How proud he was of his success.

Imagine his horror when he saw the bird, before his eyes,

turn into an Indian maid with an arrow sticking from her breast. It was one of his mother's sisters who now took her earthly form. No sooner had her red blood touched the pure white ground than the spell was broken and all of them had to leave the paradise of the Evening Star.

The young brave felt himself slowly falling through the sky as if on wings. At last his feet touched earth and he found himself on a mountain top, high above the plains. As he looked up he saw his aunts and uncles floating down towards him; soon they too were standing safe and sound upon the rocky mountain. Then came the silvery lodge, its walls shimmering with the gossamer wings of tiny insects; it landed gently on the rock and out stepped his parents.

All had now regained their earthly forms, but not entirely as before: for they were all no bigger than butterflies.

Because of the powers of the Evening Star, to bring good out of bad, they had become the mountain fairies. And the mountain top which had been bare before now grew a carpet of feather grass sprinkled with brightly-coloured blooms and blue pools of water here and there.

The fairies were happy to have such a home on Earth and thanked the Evening Star. His kind gaze bathed them all in starlight and they heard him softly say, 'Be happy, little children, I shall watch over you from the sky.'

From that time on they lived together in calm contentment. In the warm summer evenings they would gather by the lodge to dance and sing and gaze up at the stars.

And when the Moon is shining brightly you too may see the silvery lodge upon the mountain top; and you may also, if you listen closely, hear the singing of the fairies of the Evening Star.

Kaatje's Treasure

In great-grandfather's time, there stood a modest inn, The Little Swan, on the road out of Harlem to the tea-garden at Kraante Lek. The innkeeper and his wife barely earned enough to keep body and soul together; but they were happy nonetheless.

The wife, though, was a dreamer who loved to talk about the wonderful times about to dawn on her husband and herself.

One night she had a dream. Next day she kept thinking about it and was so much quieter than usual that her husband felt something must be wrong. Normally, his

Kaatje would chatter and sing all day long and did not seem to mind that they were poor. What could the matter be?

'Kaatje,' he said, 'what is wrong with you? Are you unhappy or, perhaps, unwell?'

'Oh no, Willem,' she cried. 'It's just that I keep thinking of a dream I had last night. I can see it now as if it all were real.'

'You and your dreams!' scoffed Willem. 'If dreams came true you and I would be King and Queen of Holland now! All the same, you've made me curious: do tell me what you saw.'

'I dreamed I would be rich; rich beyond my dreams. But first I would have to go to Amsterdam and walk three times around the Corn Exchange.'

The innkeeper burst out laughing. 'I've been to Amsterdam so often; I must have walked round the Corn Exchange at least ten times,' he said. 'But it hasn't made me one cent richer!' And he chuckled and chortled at his wife's daft dreams.

But his wife did not laugh at all. 'Honestly, Willem,' she said. 'I could see it all quite clearly. And I can still hear the voice, telling me how to gain my fortune.'

'All right then,' her husband said. 'If you insist on knowing if dreams come true, I'll walk round the Exchange for you – three times, if you wish. I have to go to Amsterdam next week to see the brewer.'

Kaatje would not agree to that. She had to go herself; that's what the voice had told her. And, what is more, it had to be at the stroke of midnight.

So off she went to Amsterdam. She arrived at eleven o'clock and paced up and down the Damplein (which is close by the Corn Exchange). Time seemed to pass so slowly. But at last all the clocks struck midnight.

She was very, very excited.

She walked once around the block. Then twice. And then a third time. It was quite a tiring walk, for the Exchange is a very long building.

Nothing happened.

She even began to think her husband had been right: how could she grow rich by doing this? Really, it was silly. Dreams never came true. She should have stayed at home.

Then all of a sudden, when she had lost all hope, a fine gentleman approached and, thinking she was lost, began

43

to address her. 'Can I help you?' he asked politely.

At once she told him of her strange dream.

He heard her out, then smiled in pity.

'My dear,' he sighed, 'you should not pin your hopes on dreams. I too had a dream once: of a treasure buried somewhere near Harlem, on the road to the tea-garden at Kraante Lek. Just by an inn – The Little Swan I seem to recall – there stood a gooseberry bush; you know, the sort under which babies are said to be found . . . .'

He gave a little laugh at this, poking fun at her. 'The treasure lay buried beneath that bush,' he continued. 'And for all I know it lies there still. I don't believe in dreams, you see.' Still laughing, the fine gentleman went on his way.

Well, you can imagine how fast the woman went back to the inn. She had no money left for the canal-boat back, so she just struck out for home on foot, as fast as her legs would carry her.

'There you are,' Willem declared on her return. 'I knew you wouldn't find your fortune. You're tired out, and to what purpose?' He laughed at her until he was fit to burst.

But Kaatje was not put off. 'You may laugh,' she said, 'but dreams do come true. Just you wait and see.'

Taking a spade she went to the bottom of the garden and began to dig beneath the gooseberry bush. Her husband stood, smiling, hands on hips, thinking his poor wife had lost her wits.

At first she dug up only mud and sand, throwing it aside. But then her spade struck something hard; as she cleared the earth away an iron-bound chest came into view. And when she broke off the rusted lock with her spade and opened up the lid, what did she see?

Why, brightly-shining golden coins: piles and piles of them.

Now it was her husband's turn to stare. He rubbed his eyes, unable to believe his gaze. But this was no dream: it was a treasure chest of Spanish gold – no doubt from the time of the Spanish siege of Harlem.

The innkeeper and his wife carried the chest indoors and put it on the bar. Then, putting his arm about his dear wife's waist, he whisked her off in a merry dance around the room, making all the glasses tinkle. How happy the host and hostess were!

And from that day on they both believed sincerely that dreams can come true.

Rapunzel

Once upon a time there was a man and his wife who longed to have a child. But their prayers were never answered. And then, at last, when they had almost lost all hope, their wish came true.

Now in the back of their cottage the couple had a little window through which they could see a splendid garden full of the most beautiful flowers and plants. The owner of that garden, however, was a witch whom everybody feared; and no one dared approach.

One day, not long before the baby's birth, the wife was standing at the window gazing fondly at the blooms and herbs when, suddenly, she was filled with a strange longing for the green rapunzel plant. It looked so fresh and crisp it made her mouth water each time she saw it. This desire grew greater every day so that the poor woman became quite pale and sick. The husband, afraid that she might die, promised to fetch rapunzel for her. He well knew, of course, how dangerous it was to enter the witch's garden.

As dusk cast its purple shadows on the Earth, he climbed the wall into the garden and took a handful of fresh green rapunzel leaves, swiftly returning to his wife. At once she made herself a salad and declared it to be quite delicious.

Next day her longing was three times as great!

So her husband, who loved her dearly, returned to the garden in the twilight to bring some fresh rapunzel. But this time, just as he was bending down, he saw a shadow fall upon him.

It was the witch!

'How dare you steal my herbs!' she screamed at him, her eyes flashing with rage. 'You are a thief and must be punished.'

'Have mercy on me,' cried the man. 'What you say is true, but I did it for my wife who is with child. She saw rapunzel from her window and fell ill from longing for it. I thought she'd surely die if I did not take her some.'

'Well now,' said the witch with a sly smile, 'if that is so your wife may eat rapunzel to her heart's content. But there is one condition: when your child is born it must be mine. I shall care for it like a mother and all will be well.'

47

In his terror the man agreed to what the witch demanded, relieved to escape alive. And so, when the child was born, the witch came to claim the babe, named her Rapunzel and carried her away.

Rapunzel grew up to be the most beautiful maid in all the world. But her beauty was her misfortune. For when she was twelve the witch shut her in a tower so that no man should see her and wish to wed her. The tower was deep within the forest, had neither a stairway nor a door, and had but a single window at the top.

Whenever the witch came she shouted, 'Rapunzel, Rapunzel, let down your hair.'

For the maid had long, long hair as fine as burnished gold. And when she heard the witch's voice, she would loosen her tresses, wind the top part round a window hook and let down the rest for the witch to climb.

For a long time Rapunzel remained in her lonely tower with no company save that of the horrid witch.

One day a prince came riding through the forest and

heard her singing through the tower window. Her voice was so sweet and pure that the prince stopped his horse and listened. Then he followed the music through the trees until he reached the tall stone tower. And there, of course, he was puzzled to find neither stairway nor door. Finally, he rode off in dismay.

All the same, the lovely voice had touched his heart and he could not put it from his mind. Each day he would ride to the tower deep in the forest and listen to the song.

Then, one morning, as he stood behind a tree he saw the witch approach and heard her shout, 'Rapunzel, Rapunzel, let down your hair.'

He was astonished to see the long golden hair come tumbling to the ground from the tower window, and the witch climbing up it.

'If that's the rope to climb,' he murmured to himself, 'I'll climb it too and try my fortune.'

So next day at dusk he rode to the tower and loudly called, 'Rapunzel, Rapunzel, let down your hair.'

And straightaway the hair came tumbling down and the prince climbed up.

When poor Rapunzel set eyes on the young man she was much afraid; she had never seen a man before. But the prince spoke gently to her, told of how he had heard her song, and how her singing had touched his heart. He had so much longed to see her.

Slowly Rapunzel lost her fear and when he asked her to be his bride she laid her hand in his, thinking to herself, 'He will surely love and care for me more than the horrid witch.' And she said aloud, 'Willingly I would be your bride but I cannot leave this tower. There is no way down.'

Then an idea was born. 'If you bring a thread of silk each time you come, I can weave a ladder from it; using that I can climb down and we can ride away together.'

It was agreed. He visited her each day at dusk; the witch came in the daytime and noticed nothing amiss. As the days passed, however, Rapunzel let out her secret without thought.

'You know,' she said one day to the witch, 'you pull more roughly on my hair than the young prince.'

'What's this I hear?' the witch cried aghast. 'I thought I'd hidden you from the world but you've deceived me!'

In her fury she seized Rapunzel's hair, snatched up a pair of scissors and – snip! snap! – the long golden tresses lay lifeless on the ground. Then, by a magic spell she banished Rapunzel to a far-off land where she would live out her days alone.

On the evening of that selfsame day, the wicked witch was waiting in the tower for the prince to come. And when he called, 'Rapunzel, Rapunzel, let down your hair,' she let down Rapunzel's hair for him to climb.

Suspecting nothing, the prince climbed up to the window and into the room – right into the witch's clutches. Instead of his dear Rapunzel he found the ugly witch glaring at him with blazing eyes.

'Aha,' she screeched, 'so you seek your little song bird. Well now, that bird has flown away. This cat caught her and will now scratch out your eyes so that you will never see her again.'

When he heard these words the prince was beside himself with grief and, in his sorrow, leapt down from the window. Down, down he plunged into a clump of briars whose thorns scratched out the light in both his eyes. How could he find his dear Rapunzel now?

He wandered blindly through the forest, eating and drinking nothing but roots and dew, weeping and lamenting for his dear lost bride.

So he wandered for several years until at last he came by chance to that far-off land where Rapunzel lived. In the meantime, she had given birth to twins, a boy and girl. And now she lived alone with them. As he groped along his lonely way, the prince suddenly heard a sweet and pure voice: it was the mother singing to her children.

He recognized the voice at once.

'Rapunzel! My long-lost Rapunzel!' the blind prince cried.

Unable to believe her ears, Rapunzel ran towards the cry and there beheld the ragged wanderer. She knew him right away, rushed to embrace and kiss her beloved prince. And as she wet his face with tears, a strange thing happened: two crystal tears moistened his arid eyes and the veil of darkness was drawn aside. All at once he could see again.

He gazed fondly upon his dear Rapunzel and his new-found children.

Soon the four of them left for the prince's realm where they were greeted with relief and joy. And they lived together in peace and comfort for ever more.

Tovik Tomte and the Trolls

In the Swedish village of Bolinge there was a small farm. And in a barn on that farm lived three tomtes: Tarfa, Torgus and Tovik. The tomtes were no taller than a dandelion, but they were kindly and wise, and helped folk all they could.

The same tomte family had lived on the farm for nine hundred years or more; although the farm had changed hands many times, the tomtes faithfully remained. The honour of being head tomte had passed on from father down to son.

One Christmas Eve, a party was held in the old barn to celebrate the five hundredth birthday of the grandfather tomte, Tarfa Jorikson. He was hale and hearty despite his years, yet he had recently passed on the headship to his only son, Torgus Tarfason, who was three hundred years old and in the prime of life. So Grandad had retired and lived in a snug corner of the barn between two flour bins.

The youngest tomte, Tovik Torgusson, was a mere lad of one hundred years, not yet old enough to grow a beard and only reaching to his father's shoulder.

Their home, the barn, was on the very edge of a dense dark forest known as Hulta Wood. In the depths of the forest towered a black craggy hill inside which lived two trolls, Jompa and Skimpa. They had been there long before humans had come to those parts of Sweden; they were four thousand years old.

Tomtes and trolls have long been bitter foes. The trolls were huge shaggy creatures with long green hair, icy green eyes and mouths as red as blood; they were also very stupid. Because they were always trying to harm people on the farm, the tomtes hated them: so trolls and tomtes were constantly at war. Sometimes one won, sometimes the other. It was the brains of the tomtes against the brute force of the trolls.

However, this Christmas Eve the trolls were cast from mind as tomtes from far and near flocked to the party at the farm. The barn was well stocked with apples, loaves of black bread, ham and sausage. The farmers did not mind the tomtes eating their food: for they never took much and wasted nothing – not so much as a spoonful of flour. In any case, it was a small price to pay for their protection.

Amid the fun, little Tovik called on his grandfather to tell a story. 'Come on, Grandad, tell us about Jompa and Skimpa,' he cried, climbing on to the old tomte's lap and stroking his long white beard.

'Well, my boy,' said old tomte happily, 'sit down and you shall hear how it used to be.'

All the tomtes at the party crowded round and shushed each other. Some squatted on the wooden floor, hands under chins, others sat on logs, legs dangling down.

Old Tarfa began. 'I am going to tell you how it was eight hundred years ago, when my own grandfather Tarfa Torgusson was in his prime, and of the things that happened in the forest. At that time there were wolves and bears which the trolls sent to kill the sheep and goats.

Grandfather was ever busy trying to protect the farm folk.'

'Did the trolls ever catch him?' asked Tovik.

'Oh yes, many times,' said Grandad. 'They would carry him off to their hillside home, but he always tricked them and escaped. Sometimes he brought back so much gold that he could scarcely carry it.'

'Do you mean to say the trolls have gold inside their cave?' asked Tovik in surprise.

The other tomtes laughed until their beards shook.

'Troll Hill is full of rings and bracelets, jewels and gold,' an old tomte said.

'Then why don't we take some?' cried little Tovik. 'We could share it out among the poor tomtes.'

'No, no, my boy,' said Father crossly. 'The treasure of the trolls brings tomtes naught but trouble; it brings laziness and greed, envy and vanity. That is why my father and I and all these tomtes have never touched the troll treasure hoard.'

'It must be hard to get at anyway,' Tovik murmured.

'Oh, it's quite easy on a night like this,' Grandad said. 'Every Christmas Eve the trolls take out their treasure to count it, and such is their greed they never hear or see a thing.'

'Can anyone enter their cave?' asked Tovik excitedly.

'Tonight the hill door opens by itself,' came the reply. 'But woe betide a body who remains there when the church bell rings for Christmas Day. The door slams shut and he is trapped.'

'Did they ever catch your father, Grandad?' persisted little Tovik.

'Jorik Tarfason? I should say so!' Grandad exclaimed. 'I'll tell you how he once escaped.'

All the merry tomte throng drew nearer as Grandad told the story.

'One time Skimpa had stolen the best bull from the farm. Father was very angry, to be sure; so he slipped into Troll Hill after Skimpa, just in time to see Jompa raise an axe above the poor beast's head. Father did not lose a moment: he leapt upon the bull's broad back, pricked it with a pin and hung on tightly as the bull reared up, knocking over the two evil trolls and rushing through the open door with Father on its back.'

The tomtes chortled with delight; two laughed so hard they fell backwards off their logs, feet kicking in the air.

'And you, Grandad,' continued Tovik, 'have you been inside Troll Hill?'

'Many times,' he said. 'But I've never taken anything save what was already stolen. Once I barely escaped alive; and when I did get home I was so black no one recognized me. That's because their sooty chimney was the only way out.'

The young tomte listened with shining eyes. How he'd love to fetch some present from the trolls to give to Adelgunda, the farmer's daughter; she was to be married soon. And she was so kind to everyone that Tovik wished to reward her.

The tomtes sat and listened to old Tarfa's tales for a long time, until at last they all felt sleepy. One by one they left for their own barns, and Grandad fell asleep on an old mitten in his corner, while Torgus and Tovik lay down upon a rabbit skin between two sugar bins.

But the young tomte could not get to sleep. All the time he thought of how he might bring Adelgunda a gift from the troll treasure trove. Surely there would be no harm in that? At last, he sat up, put on his tasselled cap and wooden clogs, picked up his wooden stick and set out for Hulta Wood.

The night was dark and frosty. Not a single star looked down; not a single twinkling light came from the village windows. Everyone was sleeping in the quiet of Christmas night; and only now and then did Tovik catch the bark of foxes as they hunted through the night. But he was not afraid of the dark, nor of foxes.

He could not walk fast since his tiny legs took five steps for every one of human folk. All the same, an hour later he was at the foot of black Troll Hill. Not a glimmer of light could be seen from any hillside nook or cranny. Yet from deep inside he caught a tinkling, clinking sound, as if someone was counting gold and silver coins.

Tovik began to climb the hill. It was slow painful work, and sometimes he slipped backwards, but he kept climbing slowly up from rock to rock, tuft to tuft, bush to bush, until he was halfway up the hill.

An owl hooted somewhere close at hand, but Tovik was not afraid. He made up his mind to climb and climb until he found the door. Finally, bruised and breathless, he spotted a faint light blinking through a slim crack in the rocks. Poking his stick into the crevice, he turned it slowly

and a copper door opened up. Squeezing through, he found himself in an enormous cavern with walls and ceiling of rough-hewn stone. On the floors were scattered the bones of countless cattle, and rusty swords and spears hung upon the wall. He walked on quickly.

After a time he came to a second door, this one of silver. It opened as easily as the first and Tovik passed into another hall, with piles of silver coins stacked against the wall. There was a fortune there to buy a homestead or maybe three or four. Just then he heard a jingle-jangle from behind another door.

He crept up to a gleaming door of gold and slowly pushed it open. There in the largest of the halls stood an open chest in the centre of the floor; and beside it stood two terrible giant trolls. Pearls and golden coins, sparkling gems and bracelets tumbled through their hairy paws. So busy were they counting the treasure in their chest that they neither saw nor heard the tomte boy.

On the far side of the hall Tovik spied a fountain of bubbling water that bobbed up, then down into the earth below. An old wooden troll shoe, tied to the wall with string, was trailing in the water – no doubt the troll pair's ladle.

Tovik crept up as quietly as he could, dodging behind each rock as he approached the chest. He could not see inside it even when he stood on tiptoe. Just as he was getting close, however, the two trolls sneezed, both together.

'Aaa-aaa-aah-tissssshhooooo!!!'

So strong was the sneezy gust of wind that it caught up the little tomte and whisked him through the air like a wisp of hay. And he landed head first in the chest.

He thought that would be the end of him. But those stupid trolls were too busy counting up their fortune even to notice. While they were counting, Tovik went to climb down a shining necklace dangling from the chest. But his luck was out.

Just then the church bells began to chime, announcing Christmas Day. Jompa and Skimpa at once stuck their fingers in their ears, banged shut the chest and locked the cavern doors.

Tovik was trapped inside the chest.

He would have to stay there, with no chance of escape until next Christmas Eve. He would starve to death long before that. But he was a clever lad, with more sense than the slow-witted trolls. He put his mouth to the keyhole of the chest and began to make mouse-like noises, 'Squeak, squeak, squeak.'

'There's a mouse in our chest,' the troll ogress cried.

'Let it stay until hunger kills it; it won't eat our gold,' the old troll said.

'But it might nibble a hole in the chest,' Skimpa grumbled.

'Yes, my dear, you could be right,' old Jompa sighed.

So they opened up the chest again. Imagine their surprise to see the little tomte sitting amidst their golden coins.

'My, what a funny-looking mouse!' Jompa exclaimed.

'I'm not a mouse, I'm Tovik Torgusson, the youngest tomte at the farm,' the boy spoke up fearlessly.

The trolls laughed and laughed until their bellies shook. 'Ha, ha, ha! He, he, he! Ho, ho, ho!'

'He'll make fine stuffing for the Christmas turkey,' guffawed Jompa Troll. 'Prepare the frying pan, Skimpa lass.'

'You can't eat me, I'm still dirty from my journey,' piped up Tovik.

'Hold your tongue,' the big troll warned. 'We'll wash you clean then before we gobble you up.' So he held the boy on the edge of the fountain, splashing water over him.

'That won't do at all,' Tovik spluttered. 'You need a scrubbing brush and soap; I'm full of grit and grime.'

'What a fussy little imp,' grumbled Jompa. But he let go of Tovik and went to fetch some soap and a scrubbing brush.

In a flash, the little tomte, still clutching a glittering necklace, hopped into the wooden shoe, took out his knife

and cut the string that tied it to the wall. And off he went.

The wooden shoe swiftly sailed out of sight of the trolls, swirling down into a dark and eerie tunnel. Jompa and Skimpa howled loud enough to burst your eardrums; but they could not catch the tomte now.

The fast-flowing stream carried the wooden shoe down through the underground water course and out, eventually, into light of day, close by the farm. As it bumped into the shore, Tovik quickly hopped out and made his way back to the barn.

He was scolded severely by his father, but he now had a stirring tale to tell his own children and grandchildren in the centuries to come. And how happy and surprised was Adelgunda to find the gleaming necklace on her pillow. She never knew from where it came.

The Tinder Box

There was once a soldier returning from the wars; he came marching down the highroad: Left, right . . . Left, right . . . carrying a pack upon his back and a sharp sword at his side.

Along the way he suddenly met an old witch: a horrid-looking creature with a bottom lip that hung down below her chin.

'Good evening, soldier boy,' she said. 'Tell me, would you like as much money as you can carry?'

'Gladly,' said the soldier much surprised.

'Then I'll tell you what to do,' she said. 'Do you see that dead tree yonder? It is quite hollow. Climb to the top and you'll find a hole large enough to crawl inside; I'll tie a rope around your waist so that I can let you down and pull you up again.'

'What am I to do at the bottom of the tree?' the soldier asked.

'Why, fetch the money!' cried the witch. 'When you reach the bottom you'll find a long passage with a hundred lamps to light the way. There you'll see three doors, and keys in all the locks for you to open them. In the first room you'll find a chest in the centre of the floor with a dog

60

sitting on it; the dog has eyes as big as saucers. Don't mind him. Just take my blue check apron, spread it on the floor, lift up the dog and place him on it. That done, you can open the chest and help yourself to the copper coins. As many as you please.

'If you like silver better, go to the second room and there you'll find a dog with eyes as large as millstones. But don't mind him. Just put him on my apron and take the silver coin.

'If it's gold you prefer, my soldier lad, then pass on to the third room and take as much as you can carry. The dog that sits on the third chest has eyes as huge as the Round Tower of Copenhagen. But don't mind that. Just put him on my apron and he won't harm you. Help yourself to as much gold as you can carry.'

'That sounds reasonable to me,' the soldier said. 'But what's in it for you, old woman? You'll want your share, no doubt.'

'No, no,' the old witch said. 'All I want is the tinder box my grandmother left behind the last time she was down there.'

'Fair enough, old lady, then tie the rope around my waist,' the soldier said, 'and I'll be off.'

'Take my blue check apron with you,' called the crone as she tied the rope and watched him climbing up the tree.

He let himself down through the hole and disappeared into the tree. Once inside, the soldier found himself in a long passage lit by a hundred lamps, just as the witch had said. Coming to the first door he turned the key and entered.

Good gracious!

There sat the dog with eyes as big as saucers staring at him.

'Steady boy,' the soldier murmured, spreading the witch's apron upon the floor and setting the dog down on it. He then filled his pockets with copper coins out of the chest, shut the lid and put the dog back on it.

He passed on to the second room.

Well I never!

There sat the dog with eyes as large as millstones.

'You shouldn't stare at people,' the soldier said. 'It's rude. And you'll hurt your eyes.'

He set the dog down on the witch's apron and opened up the chest. When he saw the silver coins, he emptied the

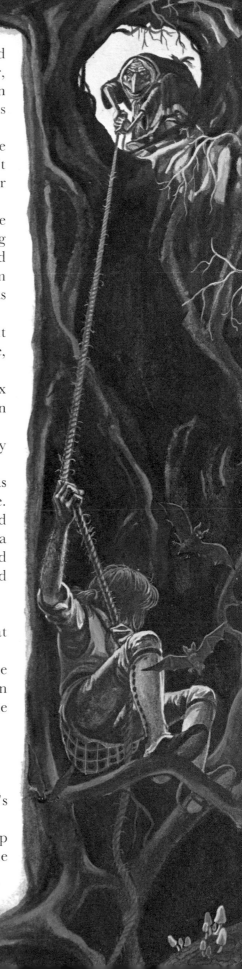

copper from his pockets and stuffed them and his knapsack with heaps of silver.

On he went to the third room.

My goodness me!

The great dog there really did have eyes as huge as the Round Tower of Copenhagen, and they turned round and round like cartwheels.

'Good evening,' said the soldier politely, and saluted. He had never seen the like before. He stood rooted to the spot for several moments, then shook himself. 'Buck up, old lad,' he said aloud.

Marching boldly up to the dog, he lifted him up as best he could, placed him on the witch's apron and opened the big stone chest.

Mercy on us! There was enough gold in that chest to buy the whole of Copenhagen – as well as all the cakes and buns, the spinning tops and rocking horses, the tin soldiers and teddy bears in all the world.

Hastily the soldier threw away all the silver in his pack and pockets, and stuffed them full of golden coin instead. And when they were full, he filled his helmet and his boots, so that he could hardly move for the weight.

Then he put the dog back on the chest, banged shut the door and shouted to the witch, 'Old woman, haul me up.'

'Have you got the tinder box?' she screeched.

''Pon my soul, I'd clean forgotten,' cried the soldier.

And back he went to fetch it. Only then did the witch pull him up; out he climbed and stood contented on the highway, his pockets, pack, boots and helmet crammed with golden coin.

'Why do you want the tinder box?' he enquired, his curiosity aroused.

'None of your business,' the witch rejoined. 'You've got your money, give me the tinder box at once.'

Her tone annoyed the soldier. 'Tell me why or I'll cut off your head,' he shouted.

'Shan't!' screamed the witch.

So he drew his sword and chopped off her head. And as she lay there dead he put his money in her apron, tied it in a knot and slung the bundle across his shoulder. Pocketing the tinder box he stepped out for the nearest town.

He soon arrived, took rooms at the best hotel and ordered the choicest dishes for his supper. After all, he could now afford to live in style.

Next day he bought himself new boots and clothing of the latest fashion. He soon looked the perfect gentleman. The townsfolk told him about their city and their king, and the unfortunate princess, his daughter.

'I would like to see her,' the soldier said.

'No one can see her,' he was told. 'She lives in a copper palace surrounded by high walls and towers. No one save the king and queen can see her because it is foretold that she will wed a common soldier; and the king will not have that at all.'

'If only I could see her,' thought the soldier, though he knew he wished in vain.

He lived stylishly, attending all the latest plays, driving an open carriage about the Royal Gardens and giving much money to the poor. After all, he knew what it was to be down and out. He was always smartly dressed and had a large retinue of friends who all vowed he was a splendid fellow, a toff, a sport – the sort of names he liked to hear.

In no time at all, however, his money was almost spent and he had only two coppers to his name. Thus, he had to leave his splendid rooms and rent an attic where he polished his own boots and darned his now tattered clothes; and none of his good old friends ever came to see him. There were simply too many stairs to climb, was their excuse.

One evening as it grew dark he went to light a candle, but found he had none left and could not afford to buy another. It was then he recalled a tiny candle stub inside the tinder box he'd brought up from the bottom of the tree. So he fetched it out and went to light the candle with a flint. He struck the flint once to produce a spark and through the attic door burst the dog with eyes as big as saucers.

'What is my master's wish?' it asked.

'Saints preserve us!' the soldier cried. 'A fine tinder box this is if it will bring me what I want. Fetch me some coin.'

In no time at all the dog with saucer eyes was back with a bag of copper coins held in its mouth. And the soldier now understood the secret of the tinder box: if he went to strike it once, the dog that guarded the copper chest appeared before him; if he struck it twice, the dog with eyes like millstones came to bring him silver, and when he struck it thrice there came the dog that had the gold.

Straightaway the soldier moved back to his expensive

apartments, purchased new attire and found his old friends just as caring as before.

But more and more his thoughts turned to the poor princess. 'How cruel that no one can see the lovely maid,' he mused. 'Folk all say she is quite beautiful; but what good is beauty if it's locked up in a high-walled palace where none can see it? I for one would love to see her. And why not, now that I can use my tinder box?'

He struck the flint and there before him stood the dog with eyes as big as saucers. 'I know it's rather late,' he said, 'but I do wish to see that poor princess, if only for a moment.'

Off ran the dog and in the twinkling of an eye was back with the princess on its back, asleep. So lovely was she that anyone could see she was a real princess. The soldier could not help himself: he had to kiss her. And then he sent the dog back with her to her copper home.

In the morning, while she was having breakfast with the king and queen, the princess told them all about the strange dream she'd had the night before: a big dog had come and carried her away to a soldier who had kissed her.

'How romantic,' said the queen, grimacing to the king.

And the queen had a palace servant watch at the princess's bedside throughout the following night, just in case it had been more than a mere dream. One could never be too careful.

The soldier longed to see the princess once again, so he sent the dog to fetch her. In the dead of night the dog ran swiftly to the sleeping princess and bore her off upon its back. This time, however, the watching servant took up the chase and saw the dog enter the soldier's rooms. Taking a piece of chalk, she drew a big white cross upon the door, then went back home to sleep.

When the dog returned the princess to the palace it noticed the white cross on its master's door; so it too took a piece of chalk and drew crosses on every door throughout the town.

Early in the morning, the king and queen, the palace servant and all the officers of the guard went about the town to find the house the princess had been carried to.

'Here it is!' the king exclaimed when he saw the first chalked door.

'No, no, dear husband,' cried the queen, 'it's over here!'

And she pointed to a second house that bore a cross.

All at once voices cried from every side, 'I've found it!' 'No, here it is!' 'Here's a cross!' 'And here's another one!'

Soon they all gave up, for there were crosses on every door in the town.

Now this queen was cleverer than queens are normally held to be. When she got home she took out her needle, some thread and scissors and made a pretty little bag out of a piece of silk; then she filled the bag with finest flour, tying it round her daughter's waist. That done, she cut a little hole just big enough for the flour to escape and leave a trail.

During the night the dog came again to carry the princess to the soldier; he loved her so much by now that he would dearly have taken her for his wife. If only he were a prince!

This time the dog did not notice the trail of flour leading from the palace to the soldier's door. And early next day the king and queen had no trouble at all in finding the culprit and having him thrown into gaol.

So now our soldier sat in the dark dungeon listening to gaolers talking of his execution the following day. To his great dismay he had left the tinder box back in his room: he had not had time to take it.

Soon after dawn on the fateful day, he looked out between the bars of his cell windows to see the townsfolk hurrying to watch him hang; he heard the roll of drums and the beat of feet as soldiers marched to form a guard. What a hustle and bustle about the town. Amongst the crowd was a cobbler's lad whose shoe flew off as he scurried by, landing below the windows of the soldier's cell.

'Hey there, young lad,' the soldier cried, 'the fun won't start until I arrive, so hold your horses. Do me a favour and fetch the tinder box I've left back in my room; there's money for you if you look sharp.'

The cobbler's lad ran for all he was worth to fetch the box – money was money, after all – and soon brought it back to the waiting man.

In the meantime, a tall scaffold had been built outside the town walls, and around it thronged many hundreds of folk, held back by the royal guard. The king and queen sat on a golden throne right opposite the royal judge and wise council that had already pronounced judgement on the unfortunate soldier.

The moment came when the soldier was standing upon the scaffold and the noose was placed around his neck. He then turned to the royal pair and claimed his right to one last request.

'All I want is a last pipe of tobacco,' the soldier said.

The king could not refuse.

So the soldier took out his tinder box and struck it:

Once,

Twice,

Three times.

Instantly, the three dogs were at his side: the dog with eyes as big as saucers, the dog with eyes as large as millstones, and the dog with eyes as huge as the Round Tower of Copenhagen.

'Help me now so that I won't be hanged,' the soldier cried.

Thereupon the dogs fell upon the judge and the council, seized one by the nose, another by the toes, and tossed them high into the air. And when they came down they split asunder, like burst bags of flour.

'Not me, I pray thee,' screamed the king.

But one huge dog shook him, and another the queen, and up they flew as high as the rest, to fall with a bang and a cracking of bones.

Then the guard took fright and the people called out, 'Good soldier, be king and wed the fair princess.'

They led the soldier to the royal coach which the three dogs pulled all the way to the town. The dogs barked with joy, the boys whistled hard, the townsfolk cheered and the guards saluted. In no time at all the princess emerged from the copper palace and became the soldier's queen; that was much more exciting than living on her own.

The wedding feast lasted a week and a day and the three great dogs, with their terrible eyes, took their places at table and supped with the rest. And, staring round, they made quite sure that everyone toasted their master's health.

Lotus Blossom

In times beyond recall there lived a widow and her daughter in a lonely valley of northern China between two snow-topped mountains. Far and wide did the maiden's craft and beauty gain renown: throughout the day she would labour at her chores and keep the household spick and span. Many were the young men who came to court her, but the old widow always found reason to turn them down. She feared living out her days alone.

Now beyond the snow-topped mountains, in a bamboo forest, there dwelt three demon brothers. They too had heard of the hard-working and beautiful maid; and the eldest brother made up his mind to wed her.

So the three demons turned themselves into mighty warriors, saddled three black steeds and, in the twinkling of an eye, appeared before the widow's humble cottage. On entering this abode, they bowed low before the mother and, turning to the maid, pronounced the time-honoured speech of courtship.

'Gentle flower, we come to court you. Untold is our wealth, countless are our yaks and horses, immeasurable is our corn. Honour our home as mistress and share all that we own.'

The old woman was loath to refuse outright such mighty warriors. So, as custom required, she curtseyed low and said, 'I thank you for the honour, but I cannot thus give my daughter to an unknown clan. For sure, you do not even know her name. But I tell you this: if you can guess her name, you may take her for your wife.'

Many were the names then chosen by the demons; yet they could not guess correctly and they had to return without the maiden.

Along the way they met a hare scampering through the bush.

'Stop!' shouted the brothers. 'Over in the valley lives a widow with a lovely daughter. Find out the maiden's name and we'll reward you with all the food you need for winter.'

Off ran the hare to the lonely cottage in the valley and hid beneath the window, straining his long ears to catch the daughter's name.

Presently, the mother began to call her daughter, 'Lotus Blossom, Lotus Blossom, bring in the corn before it rains.'

'So that's it: Lotus Blossom,' thought the hare.

He repeated it several times under his breath and ran off to tell the demon brothers. As he was running through the forest, a shower of apples suddenly fell about him and made him jump. He stopped awhile to eat a few. They were so delicious that he quite forgot the first half of the maiden's name. Blossom, Blossom . . . whirled inside his head, but which blossom it was he could not recall.

Then, in an instant, it came to him: 'Apple Blossom! That's the name – or, at least, I think it is,' he cried. And on he scampered to the demon brothers.

The brothers were delighted to learn the maiden's name and back they went to the valley between the snow-topped mountains.

When they came to the widow's cottage they declared in a single voice, 'Your daughter's name is Apple Blossom! Keep your promise and give her up.'

'You're wrong, you're wrong,' the old woman cried. 'That's not her name. Be off with you.'

The three brothers returned home cross and empty-handed. On the way they met a fox.

'Hello there, Mistress Fox,' they shouted. 'We'll give you all the meat you wish if you do us one small favour: just run to the lonely valley where an old widow and her daughter live. Find out the maiden's name and tell it to us.'

Off ran the fox, who soon found the widow's home and hid behind the door.

It was not long before she heard the mother's voice, 'Lotus Blossom, Lotus Blossom, it will soon be dark; come home and cook the supper.'

'So her name is Lotus Blossom!' thought the fox, and

skipped off to find the brothers, repeating the name Lotus Blossom so as not to let it slip from her mind.

Along the way she came to a stream; she was half way across when she saw a shoal of catfish that made her belly rumble. In her eagerness to catch them, the maiden's name quite slipped from her mind.

'The second part is Blossom, now what's the first?' she asked herself. 'Could it perhaps be Catfish Blossom?' With that name on her tongue she ran back to the demon brothers.

Once more the three brothers set off to court the maiden. And just as before, when they reached the cottage they declared in a single voice, 'Your daughter's name is Catfish Blossom!'

'You're wrong, you're wrong,' the old woman cried. 'That's not her name at all. Be off with you!'

The demon brothers stared at one another in despair and anger. But there was nothing to be done; they had to return home empty-handed. On the way they saw a magpie in a tree.

'Sister Magpie,' the brothers called. 'Fly to the lonely valley and there you'll find a cottage where a widow and her daughter live. Discover the maiden's name and we'll reward you with some golden trinkets.'

The magpie was mighty fond of trinkets, so quickly she flew to the little cottage, sat atop a tree beside the house and strained her ears.

By and by, she heard the mother calling to her daughter, 'Lotus Blossom, Lotus Blossom, finish your spinning, put out the candle and come to bed.'

'Aha,' said Sister Magpie with a smile, 'the girl's name is Lotus Blossom – mauve flower of the lotus bush.' And she flew straight back to the demon brothers.

'The maid's name is Lotus Blossom, mauve flower of the lotus bush,' she told the brothers.

'The hare told us Apple Blossom; the fox said Catfish Blossom; and they were both quite wrong,' said the eldest brother. 'Now Sister Magpie tells us Lotus Blossom. I suppose we have naught to lose in trying it.' And off they went to try their luck a third time.

'Your daughter's name is Lotus Blossom,' they told the widow hopefully.

As the Chinese saying goes, a promise from the lips must fly straight and true like an arrow from a bow. The

73

brothers had correctly named the girl, so the mother had to give up her daughter to them.

She led a white stallion from the stables, set her daughter upon it and whispered a last instruction to her, 'Look after this stallion, daughter dear; he will serve you well in times to come.'

For a long time the old woman stood on the road gazing through tearful eyes after her departing daughter; after all, she would never see Lotus Blossom again.

A black time now came upon the maiden: from dawn to dusk she knew no rest nor peace. The brothers made her

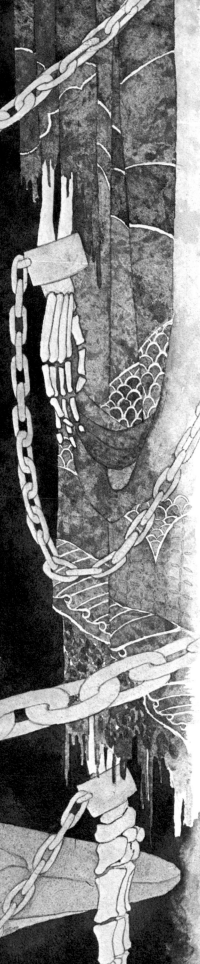

cook and scrub and mend, they treated her worse than a captured slave and beat her without mercy whenever she displeased them. And when the poor girl complained to her husband, he only cursed her more, telling her to obey his brothers' every command.

One day the brothers told the maid, 'We are going on a journey and will not return for several days. Stay home and see you keep the household clean. But beware: on no account must you open the door leading to the room behind the house!'

With that they mounted their black steeds and rode away.

Now poor Lotus Blossom was alone. She went about her chores, fed the goats, swept the rooms and set to spinning some flax. And every now and then she glanced at the forbidden door with rising curiosity.

'Would it really matter,' she wondered, 'if I just took a little peep inside?'

Finally she could restrain her curiosity no longer. She tip-toed to the door and opened it just enough to see inside. The horrifying sight that met her gaze turned her blood to ice: for the room was full of human bones picked clean. Round the walls hung torn and bloodstained bits of clothing; and among them was her own mother's shawl. She realized at last that her husband and his brothers were not humans but evil demons. Falling to her knees before her mother's ragged shawl, she poured out bitter tears.

'Do not cry, my daughter,' her mother's voice seemed to say to her. It was the black shawl speaking. 'Escape from here as fast as you can. The evil demons have gone to seek new victims. When they return they will eat you too. Make haste, mount the snow-white stallion and ride away. First, however, put on this ragged shawl; it will protect you.'

The girl, still trembling, tied her mother's shawl round her shoulders and straightaway became an old bent woman. She led the snow-white stallion from the stable and rode away as fast as the North Wind. She rode across the plain until finally she found herself far away in unfamiliar country. She made her way to a town and found work at the house of the local governor, carrying water and gathering brushwood for his fire.

Lotus Blossom never took off her mother's shawl in sight of people, fearing that if she did the demon brothers would find her. So everyone took the newcomer for an old dame.

Each day at dawn, Lotus Blossom went down to the brook for water; there she would brush her hair, take off her shawl and once again become a fair young maiden. But the moment she heard someone coming she would hastily tie on the shawl and turn back into a wrinkled dame.

Early one morning, as she was brushing her hair by the water's edge, it so happened that a local shepherd saw her as she really was. In his surprise he rushed to the palace to tell the lord.

'O great and noble lord,' the shepherd said, 'I saw a young maid just now on the banks of the stream. Her beauty is truly beyond compare; she is the most lovely creature alive.'

His interest aroused, the lord hurried with the shepherd to the river bank, yet no one was there save a wrinkled old woman.

'The shepherd has made a fool of me,' thought the

governor and ordered the poor man to be lashed.

'But I saw her with my own two eyes,' the shepherd mused, nursing his wounds. 'How can a young maid become a wrinkled old dame?'

He was determined to learn the secret.

Early next morning, before the Sun was up, the shepherd went down to the stream, hid among some reeds and waited patiently. It was not long before he saw the old water-carrier standing by the water's edge combing her silver hair. As he watched she took off her ragged shawl and, lo and behold, turned into a lovely maid with long black hair.

Quickly he jumped out from the reeds, seized the shawl and threw it into the swift-flowing stream; then he dragged the terrified girl before the lord. But the noble lord fell in love with the girl at once and was determined to make her his bride.

'You really are as lovely as a lotus blossom,' exclaimed the lord on hearing the girl's real name and story.

After richly rewarding the shepherd, the lord at once made plans for the wedding; and he and Lotus Blossom were duly married.

The lord of that land was indeed a young and generous man. He truly loved the maid, and she was very happy to be his wife; after all, it is said on coming through the darkest night, one earns the joy of a glorious day. But there is another Chinese saying: parting follows each new meeting as night is bound to follow day. And the time came for the lord to go away to war. This was when his young wife was with child.

Shortly after her husband's departure, Lotus Blossom gave birth to a handsome son; and as soon as she was able she wrote to her husband to tell him the good news, sending the letter with a messenger.

While on his way the messenger became weary and, seeing three men beneath a shady tree drinking wine, he rode over to them.

'Hey there, traveller,' cried one of the three, 'rest awhile and share a draught of wine with us.'

Now the messenger was mighty fond of wine; so he slid down from his horse, joined the strangers and was soon drinking deeply.

Drink wine and you speak many words you may regret – as the old saying goes. It was not long before the messenger was telling tales about the lord and his young wife; he told how the maid, Lotus Blossom by name, had once lived with three evil brothers, but had escaped in the form of an old woman.

The three strangers, however, were none other than the three demon brothers, whose long search for the runaway wife had led them to these parts. As they listened to the loose-tongued stranger, the demons realized what had become of Lotus Blossom.

As soon as the messenger fell back in a drunken sleep, they took the letter from his pouch and read it out: 'Dear husband, I have borne you a son, heir to your lands. Come home soon. Lotus Blossom.'

At once the demons tore up the letter and wrote another in its place: 'Dear husband, I have borne a monster with an ox's head. What am I to do? Lotus Blossom.'

In the morning when the messenger awoke, he mounted

his horse and galloped on. Finally arriving at the lord's camp he handed the letter over. The lord unsealed it, read it through and was filled at once with horror.

But he loved his wife dearly and wrote to her in reply: 'Dear wife, grieve not. Await my swift return.'

Taking the letter, the messenger set out on his return and found once more his three drinking companions along the way. Right away he joined them and was presently as merry as a cobbler.

Again the evil brothers took out the letter and replaced it by another which read: 'Evil woman, take your child and leave my land forever.'

On waking, the messenger mounted his steed, suspecting nothing, and came in time to the governor's palace; the lord's wife was there to meet him. When she had read the letter the poor woman could not understand why her husband was so cruel. But there was nothing for it; she had to leave the palace.

Taking up her child, she mounted the white stallion and rode off towards the sun. Through valley and mountain pass the stallion bore them until they came to a tree-less plain.

There it halted and said in a human voice, 'Mistress mine, listen well and do exactly as I say. Take a knife and kill me. Spread my skin upon the ground, put my bones in the centre, my hoofs at each end and my mane around the edge. Good fortune will come from that deed.'

Though she was unhappy about losing the faithful horse, she thought sadly of her son and finally did the awful deed. Then sleep overcame her.

When mother and son awoke they found themselves not on the treeless plain, but in a soft bed within a splendid mansion. In each chamber stood chests containing all manner of jewels and rich garments; outside the windows played fountains of pure, crystal-clear water and around the mansion grew trees hung heavy with fruit.

Several days passed. Meanwhile, the lord returned from war, hurrying home to his wife and poor misshapen infant. On the way he was surprised to see the splendid mansion which, he felt sure, had not stood on that spot before. Eager to learn who dwelt there, he entered the wealthy home and was greeted by Lotus Blossom with their son.

The joy of the couple knew no bounds.

They told each other of all that had passed and soon understood that the demon brothers lay behind the evil doings. The lord brought his wife back to his palace and all was as happy as before.

But the evil demons were not finished. Turning themselves into busy merchants, they bore to the palace various sweetmeats soaked in poison. By good fortune, Lotus Blossom saw them coming, recognized the eldest brother by the scar upon his ear and quickly informed her husband. Right away he gave instructions to his servants to

80

dig a deep pit in the palace waiting chamber and to cover it with carpets.

When the brothers arrived they passed through the door of the waiting room and, as soon as they stepped upon the carpet, tumbled down into the pit below. In an instant, servants filled the pit with earth and, when it was full, placed a heavy stone upon it. Thus the demon brothers met their end.

As for Lotus Blossom and her son, they lived happily ever after in the palace, with no demons to disturb their peace.

The Frog Princess

Long, long ago in ancient Rus, there lived a king who had three sons. When they were grown to manhood, the king called them to him, saying, 'My dear sons, it is time that you were wed; I wish to see my grandchildren before I die.'

To which the sons replied, 'If that's your wish, Sire, give us your blessing and tell us whom we are to marry.'

'Take your bows and arrows and go beyond the palace walls into the open plain. There you must each loose an arrow and seek your bride wherever the arrow falls.'

The three princes bowed low before their father and, each taking a single shaft, went beyond the palace walls, drew back their bow strings and let fly their arrows.

The first son's arrow landed in a nobleman's courtyard and was picked up by his daughter. The second son's arrow fell by a rich merchant's house and was picked up by his daughter. The third son, Prince Ivan, shot his arrow so high and wide that he quite lost sight of it. After walking throughout the day he finally found his arrow in a marsh; and sitting on a waterlily leaf holding the arrow in her mouth was a slimy frog.

When Prince Ivan asked for it back, the frog replied, 'I shall return your arrow only if you take me as your bride.'

'But how can a prince marry a slimy frog!' said Prince Ivan in disgust.

The prince was angry, but there was nothing for it: he picked up the frog and took her back to the palace.

When he recounted the story to his father and showed him the frog, the king declared, 'If the fates would have you wed a frog, my son, so be it.'

Thus it was that three weddings were celebrated the next Sunday: the first son married the nobleman's daughter, the second son wed the merchant's daughter and poor Prince Ivan wed the frog.

Some time passed and the king summoned his sons again and said, 'My dear sons, I wish to see which wife can make me the finest shirt. Let them each sew me a shirt by morning.'

The princes bowed to their father and went their separate ways. The two eldest sons were not in the least dismayed, for they knew their wives could sew, but the youngest came home sad and downcast.

The frog hopped up to him and asked, 'Why do you hang your head, Prince Ivan?'

'Well I might,' he replied. 'Father would have you make a shirt by morning.'

'Is that all?' the frog replied. 'Eat your supper and go to bed. Morning shows more wisdom than evening.'

As soon as Prince Ivan was asleep, the frog hopped through the door and on to the porch, cast off her frog skin to become Vassilisa the Wise, a princess fair beyond compare, and with the command of many servants.

She clapped her hands and cried, 'Come my loyal servants, make haste and set to work. Sew me a shirt by morning as fine as that my father wore.'

At dawn, when Prince Ivan awoke, the frog was sitting on the table beside a shirt wrapped in an embroidered cloth. Overjoyed, he took the shirt to his father who was busy receiving the gifts from his elder sons.

The first son laid out his shirt before the king, who took it and gruffly said, 'This shirt is not fit for a common pedlar!'

The second son laid his shirt before the king, and the king grumbled on, 'This shirt is not fit for a humble peasant!'

Then Prince Ivan laid out his shirt, so handsomely embroidered in gold and silver that the king's eyes shone in wonder. 'Now this is a shirt fit only for a king!' he exclaimed.

The two elder brothers went back to their wives, muttering to each other, 'We were wrong to mock at Prince Ivan's wife. She must be a witch, for sure.'

Presently the king summoned his sons again. 'Your wives must bake me a white wheat loaf by tomorrow morning,' he said. 'I want to see which is the finest cook.'

Again Prince Ivan left the palace in great sadness. And his frog-wife asked him, 'Why are you so sad, my husband?'

'Well I might be,' Prince Ivan said. 'You are to bake a white wheat loaf for my father by tomorrow morning.'

'Is that all?' replied the frog. 'Have your supper and go to bed. Morning shows more wisdom than evening.'

This time Ivan's two brothers had sent an old woman from the palace kitchens to see how the frog baked her bread. But the wise frog guessed what they were up to; she therefore kneaded some dough and tossed it into the fire. The old woman straightaway ran to the two brothers to give them the news. And their wives proceeded to do as the frog had done.

Meanwhile the frog hopped through the door on to the porch, changed into Vassilisa the Wise and clapped her hands.

'Come, my loyal servants. Make haste and set to work,' she cried. 'By morning bake me a loaf of crisp white bread, the kind I used to eat at my father's table.'

At dawn, when Ivan awoke, there was the bread all ready, lying on the table and decorated with an entire city made from icing sugar.

Prince Ivan was overjoyed. He wrapped the bread in a clean white cloth and carried it to his father, who was just receiving the loaves his eldest sons had brought. Their wives had thrown the dough into the fire as the old woman said, and the loaves were black and burnt.

The king took the bread from his eldest son, examined it closely and threw it out forthwith. He took the loaf from the second son and acted likewise. But when Prince Ivan handed him his bread, the king was so delighted he exclaimed, 'Now this is bread fit to grace the royal table!'

At once he invited his three sons to bring their wives to a banquet that very evening.

Once more Prince Ivan returned home sad and mournful. And the frog-wife met him at the door, enquiring, 'Was your father not content?'

'He was delighted,' said Prince Ivan. 'But now he wishes us to dine at the palace tonight. How can I show you to the royal guests?'

But the frog replied, 'Do not grieve, Prince Ivan. Go to the banquet alone; I shall follow later. When you hear thunder, do not be afraid; and if they ask you what it is, say: "That is my frog-wife coming in her carriage".'

So Prince Ivan went to the banquet by himself, and his brothers came with their wives dressed in all their finery.

'Why are you alone?' his brothers mocked him. 'You could surely have brought your fine wife in a box.

Wherever did you find such a beauty? You must have searched all the swamps for her.'

The king with his sons, their wives and all the noble guests sat down to dine at the white-clothed oaken tables. All of a sudden, as they were about to start their meal, they heard loud thunder and the whole palace shook and trembled.

The guests were much alarmed, but Prince Ivan calmed them, 'Do not be afraid, good people. That is my frog-wife coming in her carriage.'

At that moment a golden carriage drawn by six white horses arrived at the palace, and out of it stepped Vassilisa the Wise. Her blue silk gown glittered with stars and on her golden hair she wore a bright crescent moon. Her beauty was greater than tales can tell or words can relate. She took her husband's arm and led him to the white-clothed table.

The king was charmed with the Frog Princess's grace and beauty; her learned words enchanted all the guests. Her sisters-in-law looked on in envy, eager to copy her every move. They noticed that, after picking the roast

swan bones, she slipped them into her right-hand sleeve
and, after drinking the wine, she poured the last few drops
from the goblet into her other sleeve. They did likewise.

When the dinner was over, the guests prepared for the
dancing. Vassilisa took her husband by the hand and
began to dance. She whirled round and round as the guests
watched and marvelled: when she shook her left sleeve a
shimmering lake appeared; and when she shook her right
sleeve a flight of white swans swam upon the lake. The king
and his guests were filled with wonder.

Then the wives of the two elder sons began to dance.
When they waved their arms, their wet sleeves flapped
against the king's red face and bones flew out hitting him in
the eye! The king was so angry he ordered them to leave
the palace.

Prince Ivan, meanwhile, was extremely happy to find
that his wife was a clever princess. But, fearing she would
turn back to a frog, he slipped out of the palace, hurried
home and, finding the frog's skin, threw it in the fire.

When Vassilisa returned and saw her skin gone, she

burst into tears. 'Oh, Prince Ivan, what have you done! Had you waited just three more days, I would have been yours forever. But now we have to part. If you wish to find me, you must go beyond the Land of One Score and Nine to the realm of Old Bones the Dread.'

With these words, she turned into a grey cuckoo and flew out of the window. Ivan grieved many days and then, with his father's blessing, he set out to seek his wife.

One day, when he had almost lost all hope, he met a withered old man as old as old can be. 'Good morrow, young prince,' the old man said. 'Whither are you bound?'

When the young prince had told his tale, the old man shook his head and sighed, 'Ah, Prince, why did you burn the frog's green skin? It was not yours to throw away. Vassilisa the Wise grew up wiser than her father, and this angered him so much he turned her into a frog for three years from her fourteenth birthday. It will be hard to find her now, but take this ball of thread and follow where it rolls.'

Ivan thanked the man and continued on his way, following the ball of thread. It rolled on and on through a dense forest, and at last stopped in a clearing, where the prince saw a bear.

He was about to loose an arrow at it, when the bear spoke up in a human voice, 'Do not kill me, Prince Ivan, you may have need of me some day.'

The prince took pity on the bear and continued on his way, following the rolling ball of thread. A little farther on he spotted a drake flying overhead. He was about to shoot it when it cried out in a human voice, 'Do not kill me, Prince Ivan, you may have need of me some day.'

So the prince spared the drake and journeyed on. By and by, a cross-eyed hare ran across the prince's path. Ivan took aim quickly and was about to shoot when the hare spoke in a human voice, 'Do not kill me, Prince Ivan, you may have need of me some day.'

So Ivan spared the hare's life and followed the ball of thread until he came to a lake, where he found a pike lying on dry land gasping for dear life. 'Take pity on me, Prince Ivan,' gasped the dying pike. 'Throw me back into the lake.'

So Ivan threw the pike into the water and walked on. Presently, the ball of thread rolled into a forest and stopped in a glade by a little hut on hen's feet, spinning round.

'Little hut, little hut, stand with your back to the trees and your face to me, please,' called Prince Ivan.

The hut slowly came to a halt and stood with its face to the prince and its back to the trees, and he entered. There by the stove lay Baba Yagá, one bony leg curled beneath her, her crooked nose reaching to the ceiling.

'What brings you here, Ivan?' she screeched.

Prince Ivan told her how he was seeking his wife, Vassilisa the Wise.

'I know where she is,' said Baba Yagá. 'Old Bones the Dread has her in his power. It will be hard to save her, for no one can slay him. His death is at the end of a needle, the needle is in an egg, the egg in a duck, the duck in a hare, the

hare in a stone chest and the chest at the top of a tall oak tree which he watches like the apple of his eye.'

After learning the whereabouts of the oak, Prince Ivan set off on his journey and, late that evening, he arrived at the oak tree. It stood tall and strong, the stone chest firmly lodged in its topmost branches and out of reach.

The prince was in despair when suddenly, from out of nowhere, a bear appeared, went up to the tree, hugged it in his strong arms and pulled it up by the roots. Down crashed the chest on to the ground and split asunder, so loosing a hare which bounded away as fast as it could. At that moment, another hare gave chase. It caught the first hare and tore it to pieces. Out of the dead hare flew a duck, which flapped up into the sky. In a trice the drake was upon it and struck it so hard that it dropped an egg. Down the egg fell into the lake.

At that, Prince Ivan wept in despair: how would he find the egg at the bottom of the lake?

Imagine his joy when the pike came swimming to the shore with the egg in its mouth. Prince Ivan cracked the egg, took out the needle and began to bend it. The more it bent, the more Old Bones writhed and twisted in his nearby palace of grey stone. And, when Prince Ivan broke off the end of the needle, Old Bones fell dead.

The young prince then hurried to the palace of grey stone to fetch his wife Vassilisa the Wise. Reunited at last, they returned home, living together in health and cheer for many a long and prosperous year.

Pinocchio

Once upon a time there was a block of wood: just a log such as is used to light a fire. It was lying in the shop of a poor old carpenter named Geppetto.

One day Geppetto took his tools and began to carve a puppet from the wood.

'What shall I call him?' he asked himself. 'Ah yes, Pinocchio: that name will bring him luck.'

Having named his puppet he started work in a happy frame of mind. He made the hair and eyes in a very short time. After the eyes he carved the nose and then the mouth, the chin, the neck, shoulders, stomach, arms and hands. Last of all he made the legs and feet.

Then, standing back, he proudly declared, 'Nobody has ever carved such a fine puppet. Only, I seem to have made his nose a bit too long; I'll have to plane it down.'

As he set to work he heard a voice, 'Stop, you're tickling me.'

'Who spoke there?' cried Geppetto in alarm, glancing round.

'I did,' the puppet said. 'Pinocchio.'

'But puppets cannot talk,' the old man said, astonished.

'I can,' piped Pinocchio. 'Now teach me to walk.'

Geppetto thought him rather impolite, yet nonetheless took the puppet in his hands and set him on the floor.

'Now then,' he said, 'put your right foot forward, then your left, now your right again. That's it.'

Pinocchio's legs were stiff at first, but soon he could walk alone.

'See, I can walk all by myself,' he cried. 'Left, right, left, right! What fun this is. I'm going for a walk outside.'

With that he slipped through the door into the street and ran away. Poor Geppetto ran after him as best he could,

but he could not catch up, for the little rascal hopped off as fast as a rabbit, his wooden feet clattering down the street.

'Stop him! Stop him,' cried Geppetto.

But when the people saw the little wooden puppet running along, they laughed and laughed until their sides were aching. At last a policeman barred the way and stopped the little runaway; picking Pinocchio up by his long nose he returned him to Geppetto.

'Just you come home with me, you scalliwag,' the old man said, red and out of breath.

But Pinocchio threw himself upon the ground, wailing and shouting. The noise drew a crowd of idle people who started muttering among themselves.

'The poor puppet,' they said. 'He's so scared of that old tyrant who no doubt beats and tortures him. He ought to be locked up.'

In short, so much was said against Geppetto that the policeman had to take him off to gaol for his own protection. Meanwhile Pinocchio dashed off home.

'To think I worked so hard to make the puppet,' moaned poor Geppetto. 'Now look where the wicked child has landed me. It doesn't seem right.'

Pinocchio arrived home, pushed open the door and locked it firmly behind him. Then he stretched out lazily on the hearth before the blazing fire. But his rest did not last long; he heard someone call his name in a high-pitched voice. Looking up he saw a big cricket on the hearth beside the fire.

'What are you doing here?' Pinocchio snapped.

'I've been living here for a hundred years or more,' the cricket calmly replied.

'Well, the room is mine now, so just clear off,' the puppet said.

'I shall not leave until I've had my say,' the cricket said. 'Listen well, Pinocchio: no good will come to children who rebel against their parents and run away from home.'

'I'll do as I please,' snorted Pinocchio. 'If I stay here I'll have to go to school like other boys. And I don't want that.'

'But if you don't go to school, you'll never learn a trade,' the cricket continued patiently. 'I'm sorry for you, puppet, because you have a wooden head.'

At these last words, Pinocchio turned his back on the talking cricket, rolled closer to the fire and fell asleep in the warm glow. But while he slept, his wooden feet caught fire and slowly burned to cinders. Pinocchio meanwhile slept and snored as though it was someone else's feet which were burning; at dawn he was awakened by a knocking at the door.

'Who's there?' he shouted in a sleepy voice.

'It's me, your father,' Geppetto called. 'Open the door.'

As Pinocchio tried to rise, he clattered back upon the floor and only then noticed his charred leg stumps.

'Help, help! I can't get up. I haven't any feet,' he cried. 'The cat must have eaten them.'

He said that because he saw the black cat playing with some shavings on the floor. Thinking that the puppet was playing tricks again, Geppetto angrily climbed in through the window ready to punish the wicked boy. But when he saw him lying on the floor without his feet, his anger disappeared. He took him in his arms and kissed him. 'My poor, dear son,' he said, tears rolling down his cheeks, 'how did you come to burn your feet?'

'I don't know, Father,' Pinocchio wailed. 'But I'll never run away again and I'll be good; I'll always tell the truth, I promise, if you make me a new pair of feet. I'll go to school and learn a trade and care for you when you are old.'

Geppetto sighed: he would like to believe him but he wasn't sure that the puppet would keep his promise. However, he started to make a new pair of feet and fixed them on when they were done: as good as new. Pinocchio was delighted. Then the old man put on his tattered coat and went out into the rain; he soon returned with a reading book in his hand. But the poor man was in his shirt-sleeves, soaked through and through.

'Where is your warm coat, Father?' asked Pinocchio.

'I sold it because I was too warm,' the old man mumbled, blushing.

The puppet understood at once and threw his arms around Geppetto, kissing and hugging him in turn. 'Dear Father, you really are too kind to your naughty son,' he cried.

Early next morning, Pinocchio started out for school, his reading book beneath his arm. On the way, he painted exciting pictures in his mind of all that he would do: learn to read that day, write tomorrow, learn maths on Friday and, next week, learn a trade. Then he could earn lots of money so that his father need not work. He would buy him a coat with diamond buttons: how pleased Geppetto

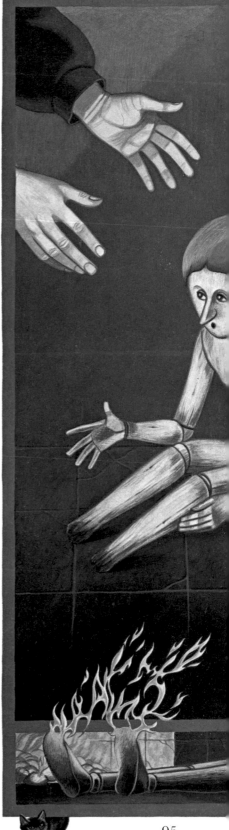

would be with him. With such dreams in his head, the puppet strode off down the street and soon came to the village square.

It was filled with people jostling round a gaudy stall; a little band of pipes and drums was playing and a big fat showman was clapping his hands and shouting, 'Come this way. Come this way. See the marvellous puppet show. Two pence only. That's all it costs. Step this way.'

'What a pity I have to go to school,' sighed Pinocchio. He reflected for a moment, 'Perhaps I could go to school tomorrow and see the show today.'

Going up to the showman, he asked, 'Can I come in, Sir?'

'Have you two pence?'

'No, but you can have my new book if you let me in,' Pinocchio replied.

The deal was made and Pinocchio went in to see the show. Punch and Judy, the Dog and Mr. Policeman were all on stage making the audience laugh.

All of a sudden, however, Punch stopped and, peering into the gloom, began to shout, 'Hey, look who's here; it's Pinocchio come to join his puppet brothers. Come up here, Pinocchio.'

At this unexpected welcome, Pinocchio pushed through to the front to join the other puppets on the stage; many hugs and kisses were exchanged as Pinocchio passed round the happy puppet troupe. This did not please the audience one little bit; they had come to see the show and now demanded their money back.

Instantly, the fierce black-bearded showman appeared, his eyes like two red, burning lamps. 'Ladies and Gentlemen, stay in your seats. The show will now begin and that puppet will be punished, I assure you.'

As soon as the show was over, the evil-looking showman snarled at Pinocchio, 'Horrid wooden pest! I'm going to chop you up for firewood and cook my supper with you. You nearly spoilt my show.'

'Please have pity on me, Sir,' Pinocchio begged. 'I don't want to die; it would make my father sad. It was he who made me. He's a carpenter, you see. He is so poor he had to sell his only coat to buy my reading book; now he has caught a cold and may even die.'

The showman, whose name was Fire-Eater, had had a father once of whom he was very fond. And now his heart

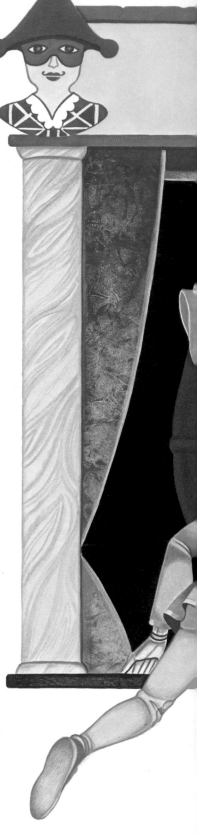

96

began to melt. 'Here,' he told Pinocchio, 'take these five gold pieces and give them to your father with my best regards. I hope he soon recovers.'

As may be guessed, Pinocchio thanked the showman a thousand times. One after another he embraced the puppets, then kissed the showman on the nose and skipped off home as quickly as he could. Before he had gone far he

97

met a fox limping along on a crutch and helped by a blind cat: they were beggars.

'Good-day, Pinocchio,' said the fox politely.

'How did you know my name?' the puppet asked.

'Oh, we know everyone round here, don't we Tommy?' replied the fox.

'We certainly do, Foxy,' purred the cat. 'We even know your father. As a matter of fact, we met him in his shirt-sleeves on the streets just now; how cold he must have been, poor man.'

'Oh dear, poor father,' sighed Pinocchio. 'But he won't be cold much longer. I'm going to buy him a coat with diamond buttons out of these five gold coins.'

And he showed the money that Fire-Eater had given him. As the gold shone in his hand, the cat opened wide his uncovered eye and shut it quickly before the boy could notice. The fox hopped up and down on his lame leg.

'Would you like to multiply your fortune?' asked Foxy slyly. 'Into a hundred, a thousand, say two thousand coins?'

'But what must I do?' Pinocchio asked, eyes shining.

'That's easy,' Foxy said.

'Dead easy,' added Tommy.

'All you have to do is bury your gold pieces in the Field of Miracles in Boobyland; that's just down the lane from here. You dig a hole in the ground and put in a golden piece, cover it with earth, water well and sprinkle with two pinches of sea salt. Then go to bed. Next morning, when you go to the field, you'll see a wonderful tree with as many gold pieces as a wheatsheaf has grains at harvest time.'

'Oh, that's wonderful,' the puppet cried, jumping up and down. 'Let's get started straightaway.'

'Not so fast,' said Foxy. 'You must wait until midnight or the magic will not work. We'll meet you in Boobyland tonight.'

With that the two beggars limped away.

Pinocchio could hardly wait until it was dark. An hour after dusk he groped his way along the lane and into a pitch-black wood. He was very scared but the thought of earning two thousand coins kept him going forward. All of a sudden, he heard the rustling of leaves behind him and, turning quickly, he saw two large, shadowy figures leap towards him. Before they could grab him he swiftly hid the gold pieces in his mouth and tried to run.

But it was too late: he felt his arms pinned back and heard two muffled voices say, 'Your money or your life!'

The puppet kept silent since the gold was in his mouth.

'After we've killed you, we'll kill your father too!' said the taller brigand who had a bushy tail.

'Your father too!' echoed the other, who had a tabby tail.

'No, no, not my poor father,' cried Pinocchio, the coins clinking in his mouth.

'Ah ha, his money's in his mouth!' the brigands cried.

One seized the puppet by the nose, the other by the chin, and they pulled his mouth wide open, taking out the coins. Pinocchio did not give up without a fight: he kicked and scratched and bit the robbers. This only maddened them even more: they tied his hands behind his back and, putting a rope around his neck, they hung him from a tree.

When the thieves had gone, the north wind began to blow, swaying the little puppet to and fro, thus tightening the noose about his neck so that he could hardly breathe. Little by little his eyes grew dim and he felt death approaching. Would some kind person come along and save him?

He remembered his poor father and closed his eyes, whispering, 'Oh Father, if only you were here to save me.'

Thereupon his mouth gaped open, his legs hung limp and, with a final shudder, his body ceased to fight.

While he was hanging from the tree, a beautiful blue-haired fairy appeared before him in the woodland glade. It was his fairy godmother. The Blue Fairy clapped her hands three times and he dropped down gently from the tree, the rope untwining from his neck. After a moment his eyes flickered open and he rubbed his neck.

'How do you feel now?' the fairy asked.

'My neck's sore,' said Pinocchio. 'Anyway who are you? And why do you have blue hair?'

'I am the Blue Fairy, your godmother,' she said.

'I like you,' he said. 'You're very kind.'

'I like you, too, Pinocchio,' the fairy said. 'Now tell me how you came to be hanging from this tree.'

So Pinocchio told his story: of Geppetto, the little cricket, his setting off for school, the puppet show and, finally, of the five gold coins. But fearing she would think him silly if he told her all about Boobyland, he said he had somehow lost the coins.

No sooner had he told her this than his nose, which was already long, grew even longer.

'Where did you lose them?' the fairy asked.

'Somewhere in the wood near here.'

Again his nose grew longer.

'If you lost them nearby,' the fairy said, 'we may find them; let's look around.'

'Oh, I remember now,' said the puppet hastily. 'I didn't lose them after all; I swallowed them by mistake.'

At this third lie, his nose grew so long that he could not turn round without hitting things with it. The fairy laughed.

'What are you laughing at?' the puppet asked.

'I am laughing at your lies.'

'How do you know I'm telling lies?'

'Because lies have long noses. And your nose grows each time you lie.'

Pinocchio was so ashamed he tried to hide his face. But there was no way he could conceal his nose. The fairy let him cry and shout for a good half hour, to teach him that telling lies is wrong. Finally, she took pity on him and clapped her hands. Immediately a hundred woodpeckers

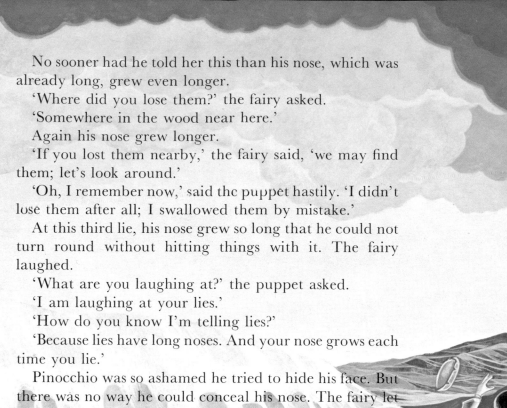

flew down and pecked at Pinocchio's nose until it was reduced to its normal size.

'How good you are, kind fairy,' said the puppet. 'Next to my father, I love you best of all. Can you help me reach my father now? He must be very worried.'

'You should have thought of him before,' the fairy scolded. 'Only an hour ago he was making a little boat to search the sea for you, since he could not find you on dry land. Close your eyes and I shall send you to him. Let us hope you aren't too late.'

Pinocchio shut his eyes, the fairy clapped her hands and, when he opened his eyes again, he found himself on a beach full of people who were shouting and pointing out to sea.

'What is the matter?' Pinocchio asked a woman.

'A poor father has lost his son and now has set out to cross the sea in search of him. But the waves are so high that he will surely drown.'

Gazing out to sea, the puppet saw what seemed to be a nutshell with a tiny figure in it. He recognized the man at once.

'Father, Father,' he shouted.

The little boat appeared now upon a towering wave, then disappeared again. Pinocchio, standing on a rock, called his father and waved his cap. Although Geppetto was far away he seemed to recognize his son, for he waved back and made as if to return to land. But the sea was so stormy that the little boat vanished into a huge wave and was never seen again.

'Poor fellow,' murmured a fisherman. 'That's the end of him.'

Suddenly people heard a strangled cry and, turning, saw a boy leap from a rock into the sea, calling, 'Hang on, Father, I shall save you.'

Since he was made of wood, Pinocchio floated easily on the raging sea, but he was tossed about like a piece of hay. It was not long before his strength gave out and he could swim no more. He would surely have drowned had not his fairy godmother come to his rescue once again. And when he opened his eyes he found himself in bed within a warm dry room. The Blue Fairy was standing over him.

'Was it you that saved me once again?' he asked.

'If you had stayed at home and gone to school, this would not have happened,' she softly said. 'And your father would be alive.'

'I am truly sorry,' the puppet replied. 'If only I could be a real live boy and have my father back, I would be a good son.'

'You could be a real boy, if you wished,' the fairy told him. 'All you have to do is be obedient, work hard at school and never tell a lie.'

'I will, I will,' Pinocchio said. 'From now on I'll be as good as gold. I'll even go to school. Anything to be a real live boy!'

'It all depends on you,' the fairy said.

Next day, Pinocchio set off for school. He had almost reached the schoolyard when his attention was caught by a boy signalling to him urgently. It was Lichinoro, who lived nearby.

'Have you heard, Pinocchio,' Lichinoro said excitedly, 'all children are invited to go away to a land where every week has six Saturdays and one Sunday. There are no schools, no teachers, no books. Just imagine: holidays begin on the first of January and end on the thirty-first of December. Now what do you think of that?'

'It sounds wonderful,' the puppet answered. 'But I've promised to go to school. What's this land called anyway?'

'Playland,' Lichinoro said. 'Children play and have fun from morning to night, then go to bed and start all over again the next morning. Forget your promise, Pinocchio, and come and join us. About a hundred of us are going on a stagecoach. Here it comes now.'

They could see a lantern swaying in the distance and hear the hooting of a horn. Presently, up came a coach drawn by twelve pairs of donkeys; inside the coach were boys and girls from eight to twelve pressed together as tightly as sardines in a tin.

The fat jolly coachman called down to the boys, 'Climb in, my lucky friends, we're off to Playland right away.'

'I'm going to school,' Pinocchio replied. 'I want to study and work hard, to make my father and the Blue Fairy proud of me.'

'Then more fool you,' said the coachman with a laugh. 'We're off to a land where sweets and cakes are free, where you can play all day to your heart's content. If you don't want to come, you'll miss a lot. Gee-up there.'

As the coach moved off with Lichinoro on board and the hundred children telling him to join them, Pinocchio sighed and sighed again. Then, with a happy cry, he

shouted, 'Wait for me, I'm coming.'

And he jumped on board the stagecoach bound for Playland.

Playland was like no other land on Earth. There were children everywhere: playing skittles and blind man's buff, riding cycles and playing ball, singing, turning somersaults, laughing, shouting, clapping, whistling. In short, everyone was having fun.

To the two friends, Pinocchio and Lichinoro, the weeks went by like minutes; and every time they met they both exclaimed, 'Oh, what a lovely life.'

Five months passed in playing: no school, no books, no work at all. And then one day, on waking, Pinocchio had a most unpleasant shock. As he scratched his head he felt two donkey's ears had grown at night; the sight that met him in the mirror made him cry and scream and beat his head against the wall. That did no good at all. In fact, his ears grew even longer. In deep despair he went to see his friend Lichinoro. But the same cruel fate had come to him as well. As they stood there staring in dismay at one another, another awful change occurred: their hands and feet turned into hoofs, their faces grew into long, grey donkey heads, tails appeared and they began to bray, 'Eee-aww. Eee-aww! Eee-aww. Eee-aww!'

They clattered round the room on all fours.

That is what happens to lazy children who won't go to school, who won't read books and who spend their time at play. They turn into donkeys.

So it was with Lichinoro and Pinocchio: Lichinoro was sold to a farmer, the puppet to a circus owner who whipped his legs and fed him hay. The man tried to teach him tricks, to jump through a hoop and stand on his hind legs; and every time Pinocchio failed, he got a sharp whip lash on his snout. One day, in trying to jump through the hoop, he caught his hind leg and fell down with a crash. When he rose he was lame, barely able to walk.

'I don't want a donkey who is lame,' the showman told his stable boy. 'No work, no food. Take him to the cliff and throw him in the sea.'

So poor Pinocchio the donkey was pushed into the sea and left to drown. But then a miracle happened: the sea water changed him back into a puppet. It was really his fairy godmother, of course, who had done that.

He swam out to sea to be as far as he could from the circus

owner, not caring where he was going. So happy was he to
be a puppet once more that he did not notice he was
swimming straight into the mouth of an enormous whale.
The sea monster sucked him in with a torrent of water and
fish; and he found himself bruised and battered inside the
whale's great belly. It was very dark and smelt of fish.

All of a sudden, as Pinocchio looked around, he thought
he saw a gleam of light at the other end of the gloomy
cavern. Feeling his way towards the flickering light, he
gradually made out a little table with a lighted candle in a
green glass bottle; sitting at the table was an old familiar
figure. Pinocchio could not believe his eyes.

'Is it? No, it can't be,' he cried amazed. 'Yes, it is, it is!'

Can you guess who was sitting there?

It was old Geppetto who had been swallowed by the
very same whale.

'Father, Father,' exclaimed Pinocchio joyfully. And
rushing to him he threw his arms round the old man's neck.

They exchanged their stories and then Geppetto sadly
said, 'This is the last candle from my store; and all my

provisions have run out. I fear we shall die together here.'

'No, we must escape,' the puppet cried. 'We can swim through the whale's great belly and out through its mouth while it's asleep.'

'You must save yourself, Pinocchio,' said old Geppetto. 'I can't go with you since I cannot swim.'

'Then climb on my back and I'll carry you along,' the puppet insisted.

Despite Geppetto's protests, Pinocchio swam through the whale's great belly with his father clinging to his back; they climbed up its throat and between its teeth. But they must have tickled the whale's nose for, suddenly, it let out a sneeze and sent them, as if from a cannon, almost to the shore. They reached dry land safely, but poor old Geppetto was shivering from the cold and could hardly stand.

'Lean on me, dear Father,' said Pinocchio. 'There's an old log cabin up ahead. I'll soon get you into bed and make you snug and warm.'

When they reached the cabin, Pinocchio knocked at the door.

'Who is it?' came a faint voice from inside.

'A sick father and his son,' the boy replied. 'We are wet and starving and need shelter.'

'Then lift the latch and open the door,' said the voice.

Pinocchio did as instructed and they went inside. But there was no one there. The puppet put his father to bed at once and then went out in search of milk and food. About a mile down the road he came to a farm and asked there for some milk.

'Have you any money?' asked the farmer.

'No, sir,' said Pinocchio.

'No money, no milk,' said the farmer grimly.

'But it's for my father, he's very ill,' he insisted.

'I see,' the farmer said. 'I tell you what: if you draw me a hundred pails of water from the well, I'll let you have a cup of milk. My donkey normally does the work, but he's sick.'

Pinocchio readily did the work and found it very tiring: he had never worked like that before. But it was worth it for his father. When the hundred pails were drawn, the puppet went, out of curiosity, to see the dying donkey and tell him how he too had been a donkey once.

But looking closely at the donkey, he said to himself trembling, 'I think I know that donkey's face. Hello, poor donkey. What's your name?'

At the sound of the puppet's voice, the donkey opened his eyes and feebly said, 'Pinocchio, it's me . . . your friend . . . Lichinoro.'

With that he closed his eyes and died.

Wiping the tears away from his eyes, Pinocchio vowed that from now on he would be the most obedient, hard-working puppet that ever was.

For over five months he got up at dawn each day to draw water from the well, so as to earn his father some milk and food. He learned to weave baskets out of reeds and sold them at the market; he even built a little cart which he pulled as he took his father for rides in the country air when it was fine. In the evenings he studied hard to read and write. For two pennies he had bought a reading book and some paper on which he wrote with a pen he'd cut from a pigeon quill and ink made out of cherry juice.

Thanks to his hard work his father's health improved.

'I'm very proud of you,' his father said. 'You've become a good little puppet at last.'

'That's because I love you very much, Father,' Pinocchio said. 'I want you to be proud of me. That's why I'm going to buy myself a suit with two shillings I've saved up. I'll look so handsome you won't even recognize me.'

And off he skipped as happy as a sandboy. As he was running along he suddenly heard a voice coming from a hedge. It was the cricket from Geppetto's old house.

'Hello, Pinocchio,' it said. 'I'm glad you work so hard. But I've bad news for you. Your fairy godmother is sick and poor; she hasn't the money even to buy a crust.'

'Oh, poor fairy,' sighed Pinocchio. 'I'd do anything to help her. Here, cricket, take these two shillings right away.'

'But what about your suit?' the cricket asked.

'I don't want it any more. Tell the fairy I'll try to earn more money to send her; I'll work until midnight every day and weave sixteen baskets instead of eight.'

He kept his promise and worked even harder.

One night when he'd gone to bed he dreamed he saw the fairy standing before him, smiling. She gave him a gentle kiss and spoke these words, 'Good, kind Pinocchio, children who love their parents and help them when they're sick deserve reward. In return for your kind heart I grant you the greatest gift I have. Always be good and you'll be happy.'

When Pinocchio awoke he felt rather strange. Glancing about him he was surprised to find himself no longer in the hut but in a bright and tidy room with flowered wallpaper on the walls; a new suit and shoes were laid out on a chair; a leather purse lay on the dressing table. By it was a note, saying, 'The Blue Fairy returns Pinocchio's kindness.'

But when he opened the purse he found not two shillings, but twenty golden coins. As he stood amazed he chanced to see his image in the mirror.

That was the best surprise of all.

'Father, Father,' he cried with joy. 'I'm not a puppet any longer. I'm a real live boy!'

Rushing into the next room, he found Geppetto busy carving at a bench, happy and well again.

As he looked up, the old woodcarver smiled and said, 'Yes, Pinocchio, you are now a boy. You have earned it by your work for others and your kind heart. When naughty children become good, they help themselves and others too.

Behind them on the hearth the cricket smiled and the face of the Blue Fairy appeared briefly at the window, a tear of joy upon her radiant face.

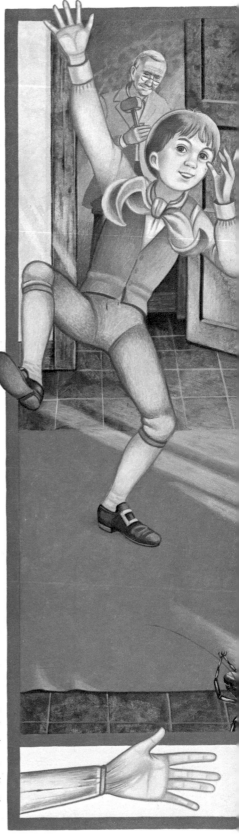

The Princess
and the Peas

There was once a prince who wished to marry a fair princess. But she had to be a real princess; there were so many make-believe princesses about. He journeyed twice around the world to find a lady such as he required, yet there was always something wrong. Princesses were certainly not in short supply: whether they were real or not he could not tell. That was the trouble. Each seemed to lack one royal grace.

At last, tired and disappointed, he came back home, very sad he had not found a real princess to make his wife.

One evening by and by, a fearful storm arose, with thunder clouds streaked by lightning. The rain poured down in torrents and the sky was as black as pitch. All at once, there came a violent knocking at the palace door, and the prince went down himself to open it.

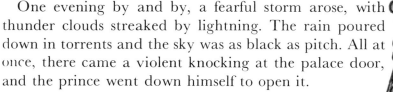

It was a princess standing at the door – or so she claimed. What with the wind and rain it was difficult to tell for she looked a sorry sight: her hair hung wet and straight, her soaking clothes clung closely to her body. Anyway, she claimed to be a real princess.

'We'll soon find out!' thought the old queen-mother, though she said not a word of what she was about.

And this is what she did to test the bedraggled girl.

She went quietly to her chamber, took all the bedclothes off the bed, and put three hard peas upon the bedstead. Then she laid twenty mattresses one upon another above the three hard peas, and twenty eiderdowns on top.

This was the bed the princess was to sleep in. There she passed the night.

Next morning she was asked how well she'd slept. 'Oh, just awful, awful,' she replied. 'I've scarcely slept a wink the whole night through. I don't know what it was in my bed, but I felt something very hard and lumpy underneath me. Now I'm black and blue all over.'

The queen-mother smiled. The prince smiled too. It was as plain as plain can be that this lady was a real princess. For she had felt three tiny peas through twenty mattresses and twenty eiderdowns. No one but a real princess could have such a tender disposition.

So the prince made her his wife, being convinced that he had found a real princess.

As for those three peas, they were put in a museum of curiosities where they can be seen today, provided, that is, they have not turned to dust.

The Little Mermaid

Far, far away, where the waters are as blue as the petals of the cornflower and as clear as purest crystal, where the ocean is so deep it would take many, many church spires, standing on top of each other, to reach the surface, there dwell the merfolk.

Now you must not think there is only sand below the ocean. Indeed, here grow the strangest plants whose leaves and stems are so light that the slightest motion of the water sways them to and fro, as if they were alive. Fishes big and small glide in and out amongst the branches, just as birds fly in and out of trees.

Where the sea is deepest stands the palace of the Mer King. Its walls are made of coral, its high arched windows are of clearest amber; the roof is made of oyster shells which, as the billows pass above, continually open and shut so prettily, for each shell contains a glittering pearl, fit for any Earth king's crown.

The Mer King's wife had died some years before and now his mother managed the palace for him; she was especially kind to her six grandchildren, the mermaids. They were all very pretty, but the youngest was the loveliest of all. Her skin was as soft and gentle as a rose petal, her eyes were as blue as the deep blue sea, but like every mermaid she had no legs. Her lovely body ended in a tail.

Throughout the livelong day the mermaids would play within the grand halls of the palace, where tender flowers grew on the walls. When the great arched amber windows were open, fishes would swim in and out, just as swallows sometimes fly into rooms on Earth. But the fishes were more daring: they would swim right up to the little mermaids, eat out of their hands and let themselves be tickled.

At the front of the palace was a garden full of trees, ruby red and sapphire blue, whose fruit shone like burnished gold and whose blooms resembled diamond suns. When the sea was calm the sun shone through it like a scarlet flower which gave forth a brilliant light.

Nothing pleased the mermaids more than to hear about the world above the sea. They would ask their grandmother to tell them all she knew about the ships and towns, the animals and humans who lived on land. The youngest mermaid thought it wonderful that land flowers had a scented perfume, since sea flowers had no smell at all. She also liked to hear about the green woods and the feathered fish that swam among the branches and sang most tunefully. Grandmother called birds 'fishes' so that the children, never having seen a bird, would understand.

'When each of you is fifteen,' she said, 'you may swim to

the surface of the sea. Then you can sit by moonlight on a rock and watch the ships sail by, and understand these things for yourself.'

No sister longed more for her fifteenth birthday than the youngest. Many a night this quiet little mermaid would stand by the open window, looking up through the clear blue water as the fishes leapt and played about her. She could see the Moon and stars; they seemed paler and larger than they do from Earth. If a shadow passed in front of them, she knew it must be a whale or a ship carrying human beings, sailing high above her. They little realized that far below them was a mermaid stretching her white arms up towards them.

At last the day arrived when the youngest sister attained her fifteenth year. Oh, how excited was she then.

'Farewell,' she said to all, and rose up through the sea as lightly as a speck of foam.

The Sun was just setting when she raised her head above the waves, the clouds were streaked with rose and gold, the silver evening star was shining in the pale pink sky, the air was mild and fresh, the sea was calm. A big three-masted schooner lay at anchor on the ocean, a single sail unfurled; up on the yard-arm sat some sailors high above the dancing on deck. When it grew dark, hundreds of little coloured lamps swayed in the rigging, lighting up the merry scene.

The Little Mermaid swam to the porthole of the captain's cabin and every now and then, as waves raised her up, she could look in. She saw fine gentlemen, the handsomest among them being a prince with kind, dark eyes. It was in his honour that a party was being held – to celebrate his sixteenth birthday. The sailors were dancing on the deck and as the young prince appeared among them a hundred rockets pierced the sky, turning night to day and so scaring the Little Mermaid that she dived beneath the waves. However, she soon raised her lovely head again and it seemed that all the stars in heaven were descending on her. She had never seen fireworks before.

Nor had she ever seen anyone like the prince. He laughed and joked, shaking hands with everyone, while sweet notes of music mingled with the silence of the night.

It was now quite late, yet the Little Mermaid could not tear her gaze away from the ship and the handsome prince. She remained looking through the porthole as the waves

rocked her up and down. All of a sudden, there came a great rumbling from the ocean depths and the ship began to roll; sailors at once weighed anchor and unfurled the sails ready to leave. But the waves rose high, black clouds gathered in the sky and distant thunder boomed. A fierce storm was brewing, that was clear. The sailors quickly took down the sails again. The schooner was tossed about on the stormy seas as the waves rose to a towering height; one instant the ship had plunged below them, the next it rose aloft.

The Little Mermaid thought this splendid fun – no storms or rollers bothered her. But the sailors were afraid. The ship's planks creaked, the stout masts bent beneath the buffeting of the waves and then, with an almighty crack, the main mast snapped and the ship rolled over.

Only then did the Little Mermaid realize the danger, for she herself had to dodge the broken beams and spars now floating on the waves. At the same time, the lights went out so that all around was dark. And then a sudden flash of lightning revealed the sinking ship. Her first feeling was contentment: the prince would come down to her abode. Then she remembered that humans could not live in water and the prince would not enter her father's palace alive.

'He must not die!' she vowed.

Swiftly she swam through the debris regardless of the danger to herself and, at last, she found the exhausted prince. His eyes were closed, his head barely bobbed above the water and he would certainly have drowned had not the Little Mermaid come to the rescue. She held his head above the waves, allowing the current to carry them on together.

Towards morning the storm died down. Not a trace remained of the sailing ship. The Sun rose warm and bright above the sea, its sunbeams giving colour to the prince's cheeks. Yet his eyes stayed shut. The Little Mermaid kissed his brow and gently brushed the wet hair from his face; she kissed him yet again and wished with all her heart that he might live.

In the distance she now espied dry land with distant snow-topped mountains glistening on high. A forest of pine and eucalyptus fringed the shore and among the trees stood a convent or a church, she knew not which. Orange and lemon trees grew in the grove beside it and an avenue of palm trees led up to the door. The sea here formed a little bay where the water was smooth and deep. The Little Mermaid swam with the lifeless prince towards the sandy beach; she laid him upon the dry warm sand, taking care to place his head in the Sun, far from the water.

By and by, bells began to ring in the big white church and a group of maidens came into the garden. The Little Mermaid quickly swam out to some rocks and hid behind them, covering her head with foam so that she would not be seen. All the while she watched the prince with anxious eyes.

It was not long before one young girl approached and found the lifeless form; quickly she called for help and many people crowded round. The Little Mermaid saw the prince open his eyes and smile at the girl who'd found him. He did not look for the Little Mermaid. How could he when he did not know that she was there? The prince was carried to the church, and when he was gone the Little Mermaid felt so sad she dived down to the depths and returned at once to her father's home.

If before she had been quiet and dreamy, she now grew even more so. And though her sisters often asked what she had seen in the world above, she never gave an answer.

Many an evening she would swim to the bay where she'd left the prince. She saw the snow on the mountains melt, the fruit in the garden ripen and be picked, but she never saw the prince again. So each time she would return a little sadder to her underwater home. She would seek comfort in knowing she had saved his life. Fondly she recalled how his head had rested on her breast and how she had kissed him. But he knew nothing at all about it.

Human beings became dearer to her every day; she

wished that she were one herself. Their world seemed to her much larger than her own. They could sail across the ocean in their ships and climb the mountains high above the clouds. Their lands were covered with fields and forests. There was so much she wished to know. Thus, at last, unable to keep her secret any longer, she unburdened her sorrow to her grandmother who knew a lot about 'the country above the sea', as she called the upper world.

'Do humans live forever if they do not drown?' the Little Mermaid asked. 'Do they not die as we do?'

'They must die like us,' was grandmother's reply. 'But their lives are a good deal shorter. We live three hundred years and when we die we become just foam upon the sea; we cannot even lie in graves next to those we love. We do not have immortal souls. When we die we can never live again; we are like the green sea grass that, once cut, withers away forever. But humans have souls that live on in the sky, long after their bodies have turned to dust.'

'Why don't we have immortal souls?' sighed the Little Mermaid. 'I would willingly give all my three hundred years to be a human for a day if, afterwards, I could live forever in the sky.'

'You mustn't think like that,' said her grandmother crossly. 'Down here we live much happier lives than humans do.'

'But I don't want to die and turn to foam upon the ocean, never again to hear the gentle murmur of the waves, never again to see the lovely flowers and the bright red Sun. Can I ever obtain an immortal soul?'

'There is one way,' replied her grandmother at last. 'If a man should fall in love with you so that you were dearer to him than all others; if he loved you with all his heart and vowed to be eternally true, then his soul would flow into you and you could enjoy immortality. But that will never happen. For what to us is the most beautiful aspect of our bodies, our dear fishtails, is to earthfolk ugly and unbearable. They consider beauty to be two ugly props which they call legs.'

As her grandmother finished and departed, the Little Mermaid sighed and looked morosely at her lovely tail. She could not forget the handsome prince; and she longed so much for an immortal soul. Suddenly, she made up her mind: she would pay a visit to the Sea Witch and ask if she could help.

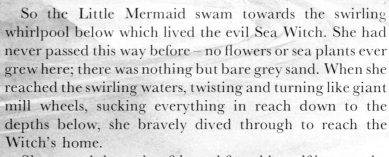

So the Little Mermaid swam towards the swirling whirlpool below which lived the evil Sea Witch. She had never passed this way before – no flowers or sea plants ever grew here; there was nothing but bare grey sand. When she reached the swirling waters, twisting and turning like giant mill wheels, sucking everything in reach down to the depths below, she bravely dived through to reach the Witch's home.

She passed through safely and found herself in a murky bog where big fat snails were crawling all about; and in the middle of the bog stood a hut built of the bones of shipwrecked sailors. There sat the Witch, an ugly toad upon her lap, slimy snails crawling about her scaly body.

'I know what you want from me,' she said to the Little Mermaid. 'Your wish is foolish but not impossible, fair princess. But it would bring you great misfortune. You want to lose your tail and have instead two stumps to walk on like any human being, is that not so? And you want the prince to fall in love with you so that you may obtain an immortal soul.'

The Witch cackled so evilly that her pet toad and the snails fell from her lap and scuttled away into the mud.

'I shall mix a potion for you. Drink it tomorrow before sunrise while sitting on the shore. Your tail will divide and shrink until it becomes what humans call their "legs". It will be very painful: like a sharp knife cutting through your body. All who gaze upon you will henceforth say you are the loveliest child on Earth. You will retain your gentle, graceful movements, such that no dancer will compare with you. However, every step you take will cause you agonizing pain, as though you are walking on a knife edge. If you are willing to suffer thus, then I will help you.'

'Yes, yes,' replied the Little Mermaid in a faltering voice, but she thought only of her beloved prince and the immortal soul which such suffering could bring.

'But remember,' warned the Sea Witch, 'once you have a human body you can never return to mermaid form. You will never more see your father or dear sisters. And unless you win the prince's love so that he takes you as his wife, you will never gain the immortality you seek. The morning after he has wed another your heart will break and you will turn to foam upon the sea.'

'I will do it,' said the Little Mermaid, pale and trembling.

'Besides all this, I must be paid,' the Witch continued. 'You have the sweetest voice of all the mermaids; you must give that voice to me in payment for my magic drink.'

'But if you take my voice away,' she said aghast, 'what have I left to charm the prince?'

'Your graceful form, your gentle nature and your sparkling eyes,' the Witch replied. 'With these you should be able to capture a human heart. Come now, put out your tongue that I may take it for myself.'

The Little Mermaid shivered, but her mind was set. 'Let it be so,' she said. The poor little thing was now struck dumb: she could neither speak nor sing.

With that the Witch took out a cauldron for her magic potion. 'Cleanliness is the greatest virtue,' she remarked, rubbing down the cauldron with toads and snails.

She then scratched her scaly bosom and let a few drops of black blood trickle into the pot, all the while adding new ingredients. The clouds that rose from the mixture assumed such terrifying forms as to fill the mermaid with horror; and from the pot came a groaning that could only be compared to the weeping of dying crocodiles. At last the magic potion became as clear and pure as water: it was ready.

Taking the magic potion, the Little Mermaid swam safely through the whirlpool and then over her father's palace. She could not enter, since she now was dumb and must leave him and all her loved ones forever. It seemed as if her heart would break; she blew silent kisses to her father and her sisters, then rose through the dark blue waters to the world above.

The Sun had not yet risen when she reached the prince's palace and sat down upon the foreshore. The pale Moon still shone above her as she drank the magic liquid; she felt it run through her body like the sharpest knife and she fainted clean away. As the Sun woke so did she. Instantly she felt a burning pain in all her limbs. And then with a gasp she saw the handsome prince standing before her. His coal-black eyes were fixed wonderingly upon her. Full of shame, she cast down her gaze and saw that, below her long silken hair, instead of the long fishtail she now possessed two slender legs.

The prince asked who she was and how she'd come to be there. And in reply she smiled sadly, just looking at him with her deep blue eyes – for, alas, she could not speak.

Puzzled, he led her by the hand into the palace. It was then she found the Witch's warning true: every step she took was like walking on a knife edge. Yet she bore the pain. On she passed, light as a gazelle, and all who saw her wondered at her grace.

No sooner had she entered the hall than rich clothes of muslin and fine silk were brought to dress her. She was lovelier than all about her, though she could neither speak nor sing. Beautiful slave girls clad in silk and gold brocade sang before the prince and his royal parents. One had such a clear sweet voice that the prince applauded her in rapture.

This made the Little Mermaid sad, for she knew that she had once sung far more sweetly. 'Alas,' she thought, 'if he did but know that I have lost my voice forever for his sake.'

Then the slaves began to dance. Straightaway the Little Mermaid rose, stretched out her slender arms and glided gracefully across the floor. Every step and leap displayed the perfection of her form and her eyes spoke far more eloquently than the fair slave's song.

All those present were enchanted, especially the young prince, who called her his little foundling – since he had found her on the shore. She danced on and on, though

every step cost her excruciating pain. The prince vowed that she would never leave his side and had a velvet couch prepared for her beside his own rich chamber.

The prince had a suit tailored for her, so that she could join him when he went out riding. Together they rode through the sweet-scented woods where birds sang merrily among the leaves. Together they climbed steep mountains and although her feet bled so much that she could not hide it from the others, she only smiled, following her dear prince up to the summit until they could see the clouds floating by below them, like birds migrating to a foreign land.

During the night, when all the palace was asleep, she would descend the marble steps to cool her feet in the caressing sea; she would then recall her loved ones down below.

One night, as she was thus bathing her poor, raw, bleeding feet, her sisters appeared hand in hand upon the water, singing sadly. She waved to them and they saw her; they told her of the sadness in her father's palace since she had gone. After that, her sisters came to her each night; once they even brought her old beloved grandmother who had not seen the upper world for many, many years; they likewise brought the Mer King. But neither would venture near enough to talk.

With every passing day the prince grew fonder of the Little Mermaid, looking upon her as a sweet young child. The thought of making her his wife never came into his head. But she had to be his wife if she were to receive an immortal soul; if not, she would turn to foam upon the mighty sea.

'Do you not love me above all others?' her eyes beseeched him, as he held her fondly in his arms and kissed her lovely brow.

'Yes,' the prince would say, 'you are dearer to me than all the others, for you have the kindest heart of all. You love me most and are like a maiden I once knew, but may never see again. I was on board a ship wrecked by a sudden storm; the waves cast me upon a shore before a holy church, and a young maid found me and saved my life. I saw her only once, but her face is vividly impressed upon my mind. Her alone, can I ever love.'

'Alas, he does not know that it was I who saved his life,' the Little Mermaid sighed. 'It was I who carried him

through the waves into the wooded bay where the church stood; it was I who hid behind some rocks, watched over him until he was found and saw that maid approach whom he loves more than me.' And again she sighed, for she could not cry.

One day a courtier announced that the prince was to visit the daughter of a distant king.

'I must go,' he told the Little Mermaid. 'It is my father's wish that I meet this rich princess; but he will not compel me to marry her. I cannot love her, after all, since she will not be as much like my long-lost love as you. If I have to marry I shall choose you, my silent little foundling with the deep blue eyes.'

And he kissed her rosy lips, caressed her silken hair and held her in his arms, so that in her heart there was already a vision of human happiness and an immortal soul.

Next morning they set sail for the distant kingdom and in the course of time arrived. They were taken in procession to the royal palace. All the church bells rang, trumpets sounded and soldiers paraded with guns and banners. Each day brought new entertainments, balls and parties. The princess, however, did not appear; she was being taught in a distant convent.

At last she came before them. No one was more anxious to see her than the Little Mermaid. And when she did she had to confess she had never seen so beautiful a creature. Her skin was so delicately fair that her blue veins might be seen beneath it, and her dark eyes sparkled beneath her long black lashes.

'It is my long-lost love!' exclaimed the prince astounded. 'You're the one who saved my life when I lay half-dead upon the shore.' And he embraced the blushing maid.

'Oh, how happy I am now!' he told his little foundling. 'What I dared not hope for has come true. You must share my joy, since you love me above all others.'

The Little Mermaid kissed his hand in silent pain and sorrow; her heart was near to breaking. She wished to die then, even though the day following the wedding had not yet dawned.

Again the church bells rang and heralds rode through-out the city to announce the happy news. Orange flames burned in silver candlesticks upon the church altar and the bride and bridegroom joined hands as the words of matrimony were spoken. The Little Mermaid, dressed in

silk and gold, was their bridesmaid, holding the train of the bridal dress. But her ears heard nothing of the solemn music, her eyes saw nothing; she thought only of her approaching death, all that she had lost in this world and the next.

That same evening the bride and bridegroom embarked upon the prince's ship. The cannons fired, the banners waved and in the centre of the deck stood a magnificent tent of purple cloth furnished with the softest couch. Here the royal pair would spend the night. A westerly breeze filled the billowing sails and the ship sailed smoothly across the turquoise sea.

As soon as it was dark, coloured lamps were lit and dancing began on deck. Her heart filled with despair, the Little Mermaid danced more gracefully than ever. Her tender feet ached with pain, but she did not feel it for the pain that was within her heart. She knew that this was the last evening she would see the prince, for whom she had left her home and family, had given up her lovely voice, had daily suffered the cruellest pain. Yet he would never know of it.

About midnight the prince kissed his lovely bride and, arm in arm, they entered the tent. All now was still. Only the captain at the helm and the Little Mermaid were awake. She stood with her white arms resting on the rail and looked towards the east, watching for the dawn. She well knew that the first pale sunbeams would mark her doom.

All of a sudden, she saw her sisters rising from the sea: their faces were deathly pale and their long fair hair no more hung down to their waists; it had all been shorn.

'We have given our hair to the Witch,' they said, 'so that she will help you and you will not die. In exchange she has given us this dagger. Before sunrise you must plunge it into the prince's heart, and when his blood flows, your legs will turn back to a fishtail and you will once again become a mermaid. You will live three hundred years. But hurry! Either he or you must die before the sunrise. Kill him quickly and come down with us; do you not see the crimson streaks of dawn? A few moments more and it will be too late.' Thereupon they deeply sighed and vanished beneath the waves.

The Little Mermaid drew aside the purple curtains of the tent and saw the bride and bridegroom sleeping peacefully. Bending down she kissed the prince's forehead and then, glancing at the sky, she saw, dawn's early light growing brighter every moment. In his slumber the prince murmured his dear bride's name, unaware that a dagger trembled above his heart.

The Little Mermaid made up her mind. Taking the sharp dagger she threw it far out to sea. All at once, the waves spurted up in flames and the water was ringed red as if with blood.

Through eyes fast growing dim, she cast one last glance

at her dear prince, then plunged into the sea, feeling at once her body turning into foam.

The Sun rose from its watery bed, its rays falling so warmly upon her that the Little Mermaid was scarcely sensible of dying. She still saw the glorious Sun, and above her hovered a thousand beautiful, transparent forms. The voices of the airy forms above her had a melody so sweet and soothing that no human ear could catch them; their forms were so light and slender that no eye could see them. They glided all around her – and yet they had no wings. Then the Little Mermaid saw that her own body was like theirs, that she too floated through the air above the foamy sea.

'Where am I going?' she asked. And her voice sounded just like theirs.

'We are daughters of the air,' an answer came. 'Mermaids have no soul and cannot gain one unless they win the love of humans. We daughters of the air do not possess a soul, but we can obtain one by good deeds. If we do good for three hundred years we can share in the eternal happiness of humans.

'As for you, poor Little Mermaid, you have followed the impulse of your heart and have suffered greatly. That is why you are now among us, spirits of the air. Perform good deeds for three hundred years and you too will gain a soul.'

The Little Mermaid lifted her arms up to the Sun and for the first time in her life she felt a tear come to her eyes.

She heard the noise of people waking on the ship and saw the prince with his pretty bride searching for her. Sadly they looked down at the sea as if they knew that she had plunged below. Unseen, she kissed the prince's handsome brow, smiled fondly on him and then, with the other children of the air, she rose into a golden cloud that was sailing overhead.

'In three hundred years I shall go to heaven,' she sighed happily.

'You may arrive there even sooner,' whispered another spirit. 'We fly invisibly through human homes where there are children. And when we find a good child who makes his parents happy and deserves their love, we smile on him and have a year taken from our waiting time. But if there is a naughty child who makes his parents sad, we shed a tear of sorrow. And each tear adds one day to the time before we go to heaven.'

Jack and the Beanstalk

A long, long time ago, before the world grew old, there lived in England a widow with her son Jack and a cow named Milky White. All they had to live on was the milk their one cow gave every day and what they traded in exchange for any milk to spare.

One day, Milky White gave no milk at all. Not a drop.

'Oh dearie me, what shall we do?' the widow said in tears.

'Cheer up, Mother,' said her son Jack. 'I'll find a job and keep us both.'

Now, you should know that Jack was a good and honest soul, but lazy. No farmer would take him on, for idle Jack would sit dreaming all day long of pots of gold and suchlike at the rainbow's end. So now his mother sighed.

'No one will give you work, my lad. We shall have to sell

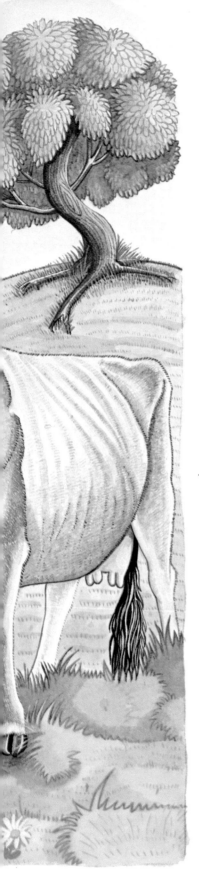

the cow to get some money to buy food.'

'Surely, Mother,' said Jack cheerily. 'I'll take her to market straightaway.'

His mother hesitated. Jack was such a simpleton that he could easily be taken in. But, it being washing day, she had to let him go.

'Ten gold sovereigns for her, no less,' she shouted.

Leading the cow along on a piece of string, Jack was already dreaming of all the gold he'd make.

He had not gone far when he met a strange old man who called, 'Good morrow, Jack.'

'God bless you, sir,' said Jack politely, wondering how he knew his name – but, then, thereabouts Jacks were as common as buttercups.

'And where may you be bound, pray?' the little old man enquired.

'I'm bound for market to sell this cow,' said Jack, 'and make a fortune on her.'

'Just so. Just so,' chuckled the funny fellow. 'You're as bright as buttons, I'll be bound. I bet you can say how many beans make five.'

'Two in each hand and one in the mouth,' snapped back Jack, quick as a flash.

'Just so. Just so,' chuckled the funny fellow once again. As he spoke he drew five beans out of his jacket pocket. 'Since you're so smart, I'm going to trade these beans for Milky White.'

Jack's smile faded. 'I'm not that daft,' he cried. 'My cow's worth more than common beans.'

'Ah, but these are *magic*,' the other said with a crafty wink. 'If you plant these beans at dusk, the stalks will reach the sky by dawn.'

Jack's mouth fell open in surprise. 'Right up to the sky?' he muttered in disbelief.

'Right . . . up . . . to . . . the . . . sky . . .,' the old man said, nodding between each word. 'And if you aren't content, come back tomorrow and fetch your cow.'

'Done,' said Jack firmly, as pleased as parsnips.

He took the beans and gave up the cow; next moment he stood alone upon an empty road, repeating to himself, 'Two in each hand and one in the mouth.'

And off he went back home, wondering what the sky was like at the beanstalk top. As dusk was falling, he reached his gate, where Mother was waiting anxiously.

'Back already, Jack,' she said. 'I see you've sold our Milky White. Well, how much did she bring?'

Jack rubbed his hands. 'You'll never guess,' he said grinning.

At that his mother smiled broadly, thinking he must have struck a good bargain. 'Ten golden sovereigns? Fifteen? Not twenty, surely?'

Thereupon Jack took out the beans to show her. 'Well, what do you say to that?' he cried. 'They're magic.'

His mother's bony hand swiftly knocked the smile off his ruddy face: once, twice, three times – until his cheeks were as red as poppy petals.

'Take that, you stupid boy,' she yelled.

In her fury she flung the miserable beans out of the window and packed Jack off to bed without a bite to eat.

So Jack climbed the stairs to his tiny room, his head ringing and his belly rumbling. But soon he was snoring like a billy goat.

When he awoke next day he rubbed his eyes in great surprise. Sunbeams danced before his eyes while dark green shadows played upon the wall. He leapt out of bed and to the window in a single bound.

And what do you think he saw? Why, the tallest beanstalk you ever could imagine!

The old man was right: overnight the beans had sprouted in the garden and now went up and up and up. Right up through the clouds.

Being curious, Jack climbed out of the window and began climbing up the beanstalk.

He climbed . . . and climbed . . . and climbed . . . and climbed . . . Up, up . . . and up.

Finally, he reached the sky and saw before him a long white winding road. He stepped out briskly and presently came to a tall white shining castle. In the doorway stood a giant of a woman – three times the size of Jack.

'Good morning, Missus,' called Jack in greeting. 'Could you spare some breakfast? I'm as hungry as a caterpillar.'

'Breakfast?' the woman rumbled in her deep, deep voice. 'You'll be breakfast yourself if you don't clear off; my man's a giant who loves fried boys on toast to start the day. You'd best be out of sight before he's back.'

Now, Jack might be a dreamer, but he was no coward.

And he was mighty hungry. So he spoke up boldly. 'Well, Missus, I'd make a more juicy meal on toast with food inside me.'

The Ogress gave a toothy smile and led him to her kitchen; there she handed him a sandwich of bread and cheese as thick as a doorstep, and a pail of milk besides. But hardly had he begun to eat than there came a great loud

Thumpety
Thumpety
THUMP THUMP THUMP.

And the whole castle began to shiver and shake to the Giant's footsteps.

'Mercy on us! Here comes my husband now,' the Ogress cried. 'Look sharp: into the oven quickly.'

Jack crawled into the empty oven and peered out at the awesome sight: he was a giant, sure enough, three times as big as her, with three sheep, two cows and half a dozen goats hanging from his belt. As he tossed them on the table, he growled – it was like thunder rolling round the heavens.

'Roast me these for breakfast, Wife . . .'

He broke off abruptly; his long nose twitched and he set to sniffing round the room. Scowling fiercely, he roared,

'Fee-Fi-Fo-Fum,
I smell the blood of an Englishman,
Be he alive or be he dead,
I'll grind his bones to make my bread!'

'Fiddlesticks!' his wife exclaimed. 'It's just the bits of flesh and bones of the boy you had for supper yesterday. Go and wash your dirty self before you have your breakfast.'

Off went the Giant to wash his hands and face. As soon as he was gone Jack went to run away, but the woman bade him stay awhile.

'The Giant has forty winks after breakfast,' she whispered hoarsely. 'Wait until then.'

The Giant swallowed the three sheep, two cows and half a dozen goats. Then he took from a big oak chest two bags of gold and started counting the golden coins. By and by his eyes began to droop and soon his snores filled the entire castle.

At the tenth loud snore, Jack crept out of the oven, seized

129

a bag of gold and ran off down the long white winding road until he reached the beanstalk. Out of breath, he dropped the bag of gold – plinkety plunk – down, down into his mother's garden. Then he climbed down after it, slithering and sliding through the broad-leafed branches. And when he reached the bottom he found his mother happily picking up the shower of gold.

'Well, Mother,' he said, 'I was right about the beans, after all.'

His mother smiled contentedly.

From that day forth they lived in plenty. Yet as the weeks passed into months the golden coins gave out and Jack thought to try his luck once more in the Giant's realm.

So one morning, bright and early, he began to climb.

He climbed . . . and climbed . . . and climbed . . .
       and climbed . . . Up, up . . . and up.

Finally, he reached the long white winding road and walked down it to the selfsame shining castle. And there, as before, stood the Ogress – three times the size of Jack.

'Morning, Missus,' said he, as cheery as before. 'Could you spare a bite to eat?'

'Go away, you rascal,' the woman cried. 'Last time I gave a boy some food he stole a bag of gold. It wasn't you by any chance?'

'I'll tell you when I've had some food,' smiled Jack.

Eager to learn the truth, the Ogress took him in and gave the lad a tub of porridge. He had only just begun to eat when there came a noisy

Thumpety
Thumpety
THUMP THUMP THUMP.

It was the Giant coming.

'Quick, into the oven with you,' bawled the Giant's wife, 'or he'll skin you alive, and me as well most likely.'

As Jack peeped through the oven grill, he saw the Giant enter, stare wildly about, then plump ten fat sows and a pair of cows upon the table.

'Roast these for breakfast, Wife!' he roared.

As he spoke, his huge crooked nose twitched and sniffed the air; and then he shrieked,

'Fee-Fi-Fo-Fum,
I smell the blood of an Englishman.
Be he alive or be he dead,
I'll grind his bones to make my bread!'

'Fiddlesticks!' his wife replied. 'It's only the bones of last night's boy inside my pig-swill. Go and wash your dirty face.'

'Umph,' the Giant snorted. And 'Umph' again, going out to wash himself.

He had his breakfast, smacked his lips, then shouted out, 'Wife, bring me the goose that lays the golden eggs.'

The Ogress brought him in the golden goose and put it on the table. The Giant uttered a single word: 'Lay!'

At once, with a cackle the goose laid a golden egg – rounded and yellow and shining.

Jack could not believe his eyes. How much he longed to own the golden goose. As soon as the Giant began to doze, Jack tiptoed from the oven, snatched up the goose that laid the golden eggs and ran for dear life from the castle.

Alas for Jack, the goose created such a rumpus that it woke the slumbering Ogre, who began to bellow, 'My goose is gone! Stop thief!'

But Jack was already scrambling down the beanstalk in a shower of leaves and feathers before the Giant could stir. No sooner had he touched the ground than he cried out to the golden goose, 'Lay!'

And lay it did: a big bright golden egg.

After that, whenever Jack and his mother wanted something, they just set down the goose and told it to lay a golden egg.

Yet somehow as the weeks passed into months, Jack grew restless. And he set to wondering what other prizes lay in the Giant's realm. So one morning early, he began to climb the beanstalk once again.

He climbed . . . and climbed . . . and climbed . . .
and climbed . . . Up, up . . . and up.

This time he thought better of asking the Giant's wife for food; he waited until she'd gone for water, then crept unnoticed into the castle and hid inside the copper wash tub. He had not been there long before he heard a terrible

Thumpety-Thumpety
Thumpety-Thumpety
THUMP THUMP THUMP.

It was the Giant with his wife.
At once the Giant roared,

'Fee-Fi-Fo-Fum,
I smell the blood of an Englishman.
Be he alive or be he dead,
I'll grind his bones to make my bread!'

(Giants, you see, have noses as keen for smells as dogs!)
Their giant noses twitching in the air, the Ogre and his wife rushed towards the oven – for they were sure it was the boy who'd had their sack of gold and golden goose. They

hunted high and low but luckily for Jack they forgot about the copper tub where he was hiding.

After a while they gave up the search, the Giant sat down to eat and, when his meal was gone, he called out drowsily, 'Ogress, my dearest, bring me my golden harp.'

That she did and set it on the table. Happily the Giant closed his eyes and murmured mellowly, 'Sing!'

And sing it did. It sang so beautifully that soon its lilting, tinkling tunes lulled the giant pair right off to sleep. No sooner did their chorus of snoring echo round the room than Jack crept from his hiding place as softly as a mouse. Tiptoeing to the table, he grabbed the golden harp and went to make off through the door when,

Clang
And clatter,
Chung, ching, ching . . .

The harp began to sing out as loudly as a big brass band. The Giant woke up instantly.

Jack ran for all he was worth: down the winding road towards the beanstalk, with the Giant in pursuit. He would surely have been caught had not the Giant stumbled once or twice, tripping over his lanky legs. All the same, when Jack reached the beanstalk, the Giant was only a dozen paces behind.

Down scrambled Jack, the singing harp beneath his arm. And down too came the Giant – though not as fast as Jack, since he was so big and clumsy.

When Jack's cottage came in sight, he shouted to his mother, 'Quick, quick, bring an axe.'

As luck would have it, his mother had been chopping wood and held the chopper ready for her son. But then she almost swooned in fright: for two giant legs were descending through the clouds.

As Jack touched earth, he seized the axe and swung it back and forth, biting into the solid stalk. The beanstalk began to bend and sway like a corn ear in the breeze. And finally it toppled over with the Giant half way down.

CRASH – the Giant burst apart like a bag of peas.

After clearing up the mess, Jack and his mother lived in peace and plenty. No more did they lack for food or fun. For now they had the goose that laid the golden eggs and the harp that sang such lovely songs.

Children of the Wind

Have you noticed how the Wind grows still as twilight falls? All day long he runs over seas and islands; he hunts within the forest and scours the desert, driving herds of timid deer towards the waterholes. Through all the hours of daylight he refreshes the mountain, supports the bird's wing and brings to all lands tidings of the changing seasons.

Such are the duties of the Wind.

But of an evening, when he is tired of travelling, he folds his wings and sinks down as the red Sun sets. He floats below the clouds, hovers just a moment as he chooses a sand-dune or a clearing, then settles down.

The great bushland knows the Wind's close secrets; she knows that every night Wind takes the form of a bird or wild beast, so as to slumber undisturbed. Asleep, he looks so beautiful.

'Hush, the Wind is sleeping,' the bushland whispers to her children.

The green parrot on the bough – that is the Wind.

The silver lizard coiled in a strip of moonlight on the hillside – that is the Wind.

Over by the Niger at Lake Debo you may see just above the pale horizon a flight of pink flamingoes – that is the Wind alighting on the water.

It sometimes happens that he goes to sleep close by a village; he stretches out tall and handsome in the grass and slumbers with his head cradled on one arm.

So it was one time when Aminata, a young maid of Maca, who had gone to fetch water, found Wind sleeping beneath a tree and stopped to look at him. She took him for a traveller, a stranger from some other land: he was the hero of her dreams, the very man she had sought since love awakened in her breast.

Dust and sweat streaked his head and eyelids, and on his body were scratches and open cuts. His tired mouth puckered softly as he slept. With gentle, timid hands the girl cleaned his wounds and bathed his eyes and forehead.

It was a beautiful night for the mysterious meeting of Aminata and the stranger with the copper-coloured hair; the full Moon shone brightly down. So overwhelmed with love was she that the maid did not hear the old fisherman Abbege poling his way back from Gorom and then grumbling as he staggered up the path, bent beneath his bundle of nets and lines.

The old man used to listen to the Wind and hold conversations with him. 'Frish. Frish!' he would call.

But that night the fisherman had no reply. As twilight fell, at the time when White Eagle's call down in the mangrove swamps is the signal to the tides to change the currents, Abbege had shouted to the Wind as usual on his journey home.

He put up the sail of his dhow and shouted loudly, towards the south, 'Frish. Frish! Come to me, my little breeze.'

He called again on a bamboo whistle whose notes carried far and fell with a dull sound like beads. But the river rose and Abbege's sail flapped against the mast. Chewing his tobacco quid, he poled his dhow down to Maca against the full force of the tide.

'The Wind must be getting deaf,' he grumbled.

At that very moment the Wind, clad all in blue, was still lying sleeping under the tree of Maca where the River Senegal meanders through the sand-banks and rests before flowing out to the sea. Aminata sat fondly watching over him. Here he was to return for several days – and those were days which the Lebu fisherfolk in their round huts

and the Pulo shepherds in their oxhide tents were to remember for a long, long time to come.

Out of a tree dived a toucan at dawn's first light; the parrot's eye blushed pink, and a guinea-fowl stretched its neck and went in search of seeds. There was a rustling in the trees as all the animals woke up. With a sudden sigh of surprise the wide expanse of open country awoke to morning. The turtledove's first cooing expressed the thrill of the new day in clear and limpid notes.

Wind opened his eyes and saw above him a maiden's face with such a tender look. 'What is your name?' he asked.

'Aminata,' the girl replied.

'And your village?'

'Maca on the river,' she said.

'And who was the first boy in your village to tell you you are beautiful?'

The girl was silent.

'You do not reply, Aminata.'

'I love to hear you speak my name,' she sighed.

'It is as fresh as the water in your pitcher.'

She lowered her eyes and held out the jug for him that he might drink. He took a long draught.

She dared to address him now since he was no longer looking at her face. 'I have long awaited a stranger sleeping beneath this tree,' she murmured. 'A stranger such as you.'

For a moment he was pensive. Then Wind gently said, 'Aminata, in my wanderings, I too have often dreamed. My dream was of a beautiful daughter of the People who was just like you. But I am a wanderer; I never halt. I am from here and there and everywhere where I am not. Yet, somehow I long now to stay with you. I often grow tired of running to and fro about the world.'

'But who makes you do so?' Aminata asked.

'I have to do my duty. You do not understand.'

The morning rhythm of the pestles beat out as the women pounded millet before their huts. Abbege meanwhile unhooked his nets and set off towards the river once again.

As he passed by the couple he was still muttering like the night before, 'Wind is getting old and deaf.'

When he reached the end of the path they heard him calling Wind as he unfurled his patched white sail. Then the stranger rose, as light as dandelion fluff, gazed long into the girl's deep violet eyes, as if making a promise to her, and said, 'Frish. That's what they call me.'

A deep-throated laugh burst from him and his white teeth flashed. 'Well, I must accompany this fisherman who's bound for Gorom. He calls my name and I must help him move upstream. He thinks I'm old and deaf. But, oh, Aminata, Wind is not deaf, Wind has the sharpest ears.'

She did not dare to ask him when he would return. But he guessed the question in her eyes. 'I shall be back, Aminata.'

'Then I shall wait for you,' she said.

'This evening, under the selfsame tree.'

'Will you be able to find the way back?' whispered Aminata, getting anxious.

'Yes, I know every way and byway of the world,' said the stranger with a hearty laugh, 'and I would find you again even if I had to travel to Earth's end.'

With that he vanished into the distance.

All day long her thoughts dwelt on this dreamlike meeting which she could hardly believe was true, and yet she had his promise singing in her heart. When evening came she was waiting beneath the tree.

With the first trembling touch of night, as the last breath of Wind stirred the lower boughs, he came to her, bending the grass and raising a puff of dust to tickle the house dogs' noses as they sat before the huts biting and scratching their mangy coats.

Aminata brought him home to her family in their hut, where laughing children got under everybody's feet; and then, when her father was back from hunting, they all sat down to a tasty meal, Wind eating with his fingers like a man and drinking *dolo* beer as he related his travels and adventures. By and by, the village elders came and listened to his words.

There was long discussion that night in Aminata's hut. For Wind had chosen her to be his wife, yet did not even bargain over the bride-price asked in token of the agreement. But, after all, he was a great and noble lord.

That night, as everyone in the hut was sleeping, Wind rose and left. The thorn-trees in the forest shook violently as he took flight: he sought far distant lands, each with its own fruit and flowers and beasts, and he returned to Maca at daybreak laden down like a king with presents.

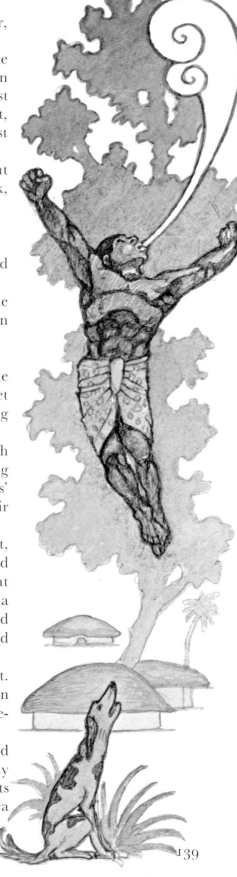

The wedding celebrations began that day. It was a time of great rejoicing. The grasshoppers sang in tune with birds from all the islands. The river brought its fish and guinea-fowl to the banks; the forest gave them doe and bustard.

Up in the clear blue sky, the Sun stifled its fire for the birds who flew above the happy village, making silhouettes and patterns in the sky. There was so much feasting and drinking that the day is still remembered in the thatched mud huts on the banks of the River Senegal.

The newly-married traveller remained by their hearth and his bride until the next new Moon. Then he began to be restless, putting his ear outside to catch a message on the heavy air at noon or dusk when the little bells of silence sound.

'I shall have to go,' he said one day to Aminata. 'They are waiting for me.'

'Who is waiting?' she asked, surprised.

'The rains.'

'You are hiding something from me, aren't you?' she enquired.

'I must, I fear.'

'Won't you even tell your wife?' she said in tears.

'I cannot tell it to a soul.'

'Then why tell me false, that the rains are waiting for you?'

'But that is true, Aminata. The herring gulls have told me. I must open the way for the new season, warn the village elders who already feel it in their bones; I must act as herald to the fertile lands. And I am already late. Farewell, Aminata. It will not be long before I'm back. I'll take you by surprise one evening, when my day's work is done. I shall come for you beside the water where I first met you.'

'Will you send me news?' she asked.

'Yes, I shall, by the fisherman Abbege who knows my name; and of an evening I will talk to you through the trees, caress you in the soft dawn breeze. You will hear me singing in the boughs, "Frish, frish!"'

'Frish,' murmured the girl fondly.

That is how Wind took a wife and in the passing of the years had three fine children. The first child was a boy named Mamadu Marta, the second a girl, by name Binetu; the last born was a second son, Alama.

Never were children seen so lithe and light as they were.

In the meadows where the washerwomen spread their linen on the grass to dry they would rush about until they were quite out of breath; every time they passed, they made the clothes blow to and fro. They would wander through the forest, blowing with all their might into the bushes, putting to flight the dune partridge and leading deer astray with their mischievous gusts of wind. The eldest, whose lungs were like a blacksmith's bellows, would accompany old Abbege to the fishing grounds.

'Frish, frish!' the old fisherman would cry.

And Mamadu Marta would come rushing over the horizon, leaping into the dhow's stern and blowing the sail fit to tear the canvas.

Binetu learned singing from birds and crickets and would sing for hours as she walked through fields of flowers, gathering golden sunbeams and scattering them to the breeze. Her breath was fragrant with thyme and mint and mayflower. In Aminata's garden there grew pretty flowers which her daughter brought from far and near, and encouraged to grow with her songs.

Her father called the songs the Wind of Flowers, when his journeys brought him to the People's village and he stayed there for a while. Then Aminata was so happy. He would spend a night with her and tell the little ones stories from the Lands of the Orange Sunset. Throughout the long night, boats would be becalmed on the still sea, dead leaves would never fall from branches and over the world reigned an eerie silence which soil, water and grass all found hard to bear – except at Maca where it seemed but a short pause before Wind began another story to his children and blew gently on the embers in the hearth.

For a few years Wind had come back at every change of season. And then, when Aminata was awaiting her third child, between the rains and the arid season, Wind did not come. The Sun burned down upon the bushland, yet at Maca there was still no sign of the foot-weary wanderer. This was the time when in a distant land across the seas, where the dragon is the royal beast, there was much misery and countless wrecks at sea, and a great flood which wore away the Earth right down to the bed rock. In that dragon country, Wind used up his anger at having to stay while they were waiting for him in Maca.

Until the end Aminata still hoped to see the one who had forsaken the love of the People's daughter, and she died

after giving birth to her third child, the most beautiful of all. He had deep black eyes, almost violet in colour, and his laugh was soft and wistful like his mother's.

Aminata held him to her breast till her last breath, talking to him as if he could understand – as no doubt he did – telling him the prayer which eases death, yet still hoping for a miracle that would bring back her husband whom she loved so dearly.

All that long night of waiting Abbege stayed by the river bank, calling, 'Frish, frish! Come, come,' as if he knew the secret of the Wind and Aminata.

'He will surely come,' thought Aminata, looking at her baby. 'My baby, my little baby, who will never know me, do you sense the pain that's in my heart? Tonight it beats with all the sorrow of the world; its echo runs all through my body. Listen. How sadly the Wind moans outside. From far away he brings the cry of all who suffer here on Earth. My little baby, remember later, when you're a man: I can feel within me everything that suffers and dies without a comfort. Oh, my son, how long the Wind is in coming.'

Deep suffering opens up the heart; that is what made the third child of the Wind so tender-hearted.

Old Abbege reported later that towards the dawn he saw a big white seagull pass low over the water issuing a heart-rending cry and heading for the village. When he went up to the village and pushed open Aminata's door, he swore he saw the seagull standing on one leg and looking at the child.

This is what he heard, 'You have come back, handsome nomad of my dreams. I grieve no longer, now that you are here.'

'Yes, I am here, Aminata.'

'My suffering is at an end,' she sighed. 'The world for me falls silent. How deeply I have suffered all this night.'

'Every night and every day, dear Aminata.'

'Farewell, Frish, I love you dearly,' were her last words.

Abbege never doubted for a moment that the white seagull was the Wind who, unable to change his shape in time, had come winging to Aminata to bring her one last ray of joy. Then the old man began calling through the village.

'Women, Aminata is dead. Do you not hear across the bush the singing of the reed-pipes, drums and wooden flutes? Misfortune has come. Go, women, to Aminata's – there is a baby crying.'

In the villages of that land there is a custom that if a baby's mother dies, the nearest neighbour must fetch the child and bring it up as if it were her own.

'We'll call him Alama,' said the weaver's wife, as she wrapped him in her cloth.

Meanwhile, the white seagull circled for some moments above the village, then turned and flew straight out to sea.

Wind's second son grew up a sturdy boy. His childhood was that of any normal child in a river village, save that he

used not to play with other children of his age. He liked to wander by himself within the jungle, befriending baby birds who'd fallen from their nests. He was a lonely boy, yet kind and gentle. For if he came upon an ailing person stretched out upon a straw bed, he always had a word that brought a gleam of joy into the eyes. Alama's words soothed pain like balm; he knew the flowers in Binetu's garden whose roots had power to put pain to sleep and quieten the soul.

River Wind, Flower Wind, and Wind of Mercy. These were the names of Wind's three children. All of them one day flew away from their village home. To the first, Wind of the Rivers, his father gave the realm of meandering brooks, rivers, streams and swamps. Old Abbege's sons always whistle for him when the kingfisher calls. The girl Binetu, Wind of the Flowers, haunts the fields and woods, and everywhere she goes she brings warm spring days, fruit in autumn, and on hot days, when the air shimmers in the sun, it is she who tosses up those little glittering grains of gold which are neither flower nor insect.

Alama, the last, has the most beautiful realm of all. He gently rocks and comforts and lulls the sadness of the world, he sings for those who mourn, he brings a breath of joy and a soothing caress. It is he who gives the signal for the prayers of People down on Earth.

Do not refuse to sing for him when, in a soft whisper, he seeks your help to cheer the sick and poor.

The Fisherman of Kinsale

There was once an Irish fisherman from Kinsale who had seven sons. He was very poor; many's the time he and his wife and children had not a bite to eat for days on end. Whenever his nets were empty he had to comb the beach for shellfish.

One day as he was unhappily sailing home with empty nets, he saw a fair sight to astound the eyes: a beautiful mermaid was rising from the sea. He dropped anchor as she swam towards him.

'Poor fisherman,' she said, 'let me help you. I'll bring you fish and much besides, save your family from starvation and make you rich. But you must give me one thing in return: when your eldest son is twenty-one, he must be mine.'

The fisherman twisted his grey moustache and scratched his head. At last, rather than return home with no fish, he consented to the deal. And when he finally came ashore his children were waiting on the sand, wondering what had kept him. They were amazed to see the big basketfuls of fine fresh fish inside his boat. Such a catch had he that he sent his children off to take some baskets to his friends. And the friends, in turn, sent back oatmeal cakes, poteen and baked potato pies, so that he now had food and drink of every kind.

Every day thenceforth he caught the best of all the fish there was. Soon he had cash enough to buy a farm, and then a second and a third, until he came to own a pretty village. He even sent his seven boys to school. And well he could afford it, for the mermaid brought him pearls and coral besides the fish. After that, he bought fine horses with leather saddles for his sons to ride about the lands of County Cork, like sons of gentlemen.

But time fast brought repayment near: his eldest son Sean would shortly have to go. The father grew so sick that he took to his bed and would not eat or drink. He had never revealed his secret to his wife or sons, and they knew nothing of the pact.

One morning, Sean stood by his father's bed, begging to

know what ailed him. And when his father would not say, he vowed to leave the house forever if the secret was not shared.

'My son, 'twould be better for you not to know,' his father said. 'But if you will go from us afore I tell it, then 'tis sure you ought to know.' And he told Sean all there was to tell from start to end.

'Never mind, Father,' said Sean at last. 'Even should I go you'll have six sons left. I'll do for myself right enough; now give me your blessing and I'll make away to seek my fortune.'

The father gave his blessing and Sean rode away.

He journeyed on until he came to a quiet strand; and as he rode along it he saw a hedgehog, bear and hawk all quarrelling over the carcass of a sheep.

'A hundred thousand welcomes to you, Sean, son of the Fisherman of Kinsale,' they called. 'We have a quarrel here; will you settle it for us?'

'I'll do so, willingly,' said Sean.

Making three parts of the carcass, he gave the body to the bear, the sheep's head to the hawk, and the entrails to the hedgehog.

Each was mighty satisfied. As Sean turned to go, the bear called to him, 'Should you ever be in need, just call my name and you'll become a bear at once.'

The hawk spoke next, 'Whenever you're in need of help from me, just speak my name and you'll become a hawk.'

The hedgehog made his gift likewise, and Sean rode away, eager to try out the three strange powers he had now acquired.

Dismounting from his horse, he summoned up the hawk and wished for its form and flying power. Straightaway he turned into a hawk, one of the finest birds to grace man's eyes. He soared into the sky, flew across the sea to the opposite shore and rested a while before flying on.

On the following day, he spied below three princesses travelling in the royal carriage to a fair. Since they seemed right fair colleens, he fluttered round their coach to take a better look. But the eldest sister seized him by the tail and pulled him down.

'I'll take this fine bird home and put him in a cage,' she told her sisters.

Thus, when the coach came to the fair, she shut him up inside the carriage awaiting her return. Imagine her surprise to find, instead of a hawk, a handsome fellow sitting on her seat when she came back. It was, of course, none other than Sean the fisherman's son, returned to human form. The young lady fell in love at once, thinking him the handsomest man she'd ever seen. He, too, was enchanted by the lady's beauty and asked how he might win her hand.

'In three days' time,' she said, 'many great champions are coming to my father's castle to seek a bride. This is how they hope to win: there is a high wall round my father's castle topped by great sharp spikes. My father has said that he who can leap across the castle wall, both in and out again, can wed the daughter of his choice.'

And so it was. On the day of the trial many champions came from round the world to assemble in the courtyard. Every man who fancied he could jump was there to seek his fortune. From the topmost tower of the castle, the three lovely sisters gazed down on them.

At last the hour arrived for the trial to start. The first bold fellows did not reach even half way up the wall and fell back with a crash. Next, some reached the top but landed on the great sharp spikes that pierced their bodies through. Many a brave man perished thus.

Finally it was the turn of Sean. Taking a run so long it almost put him out of sight, he swiftly changed into a hawk and soared lightly over the castle wall and back again. A great cheer went up at this astounding feat, and Sean claimed the eldest daughter for his bride.

Seven days of feasting were declared to celebrate the wedding. But on the third day, Sean grew uneasy because it was his birthday: he was twenty-one. And he recalled his father's pledge. His worry soon turned to fear. For in the middle of the wedding feast the castle doors flew open and in came the most horrid-looking hag, no longer disguised as a beautiful mermaid but all dressed in green, wet seaweed dripping from her hair. Before anyone could move, she had snatched up Sean and, rising through the air, flew off with him towards her watery realm.

All present in the castle saw and wondered at this sorcery. But Sean's new bride was not a maid to sit and weep. She swiftly saddled up her horse and rode off like the wind in pursuit of her beloved husband. She followed all through the day and, towards evening, saw the green hag, with Sean, drop down to the sea and sink into the water.

The newly-married maid halted sadly on the shore, lamenting to the waves, 'Give me back my husband, you've no right to take him.'

By and by, the old hag appeared out of the deep.

'Give back my husband,' called the young wife again. 'I'll gladly take his place if you will spare him.'

The hag rose from the sea and, leaping high, she landed on the shore with Sean, as dry as if he'd never been near water. Releasing the frightened lad, she snatched up the maiden and returned with her to the watery depths.

Sean called and cried, but not a sign of his wife or the sea hag could be seen. In the pale rays of dawn he lay down to sleep exhausted upon the sandy shore. When he awoke it was already getting dark, and straining his eyes he could see a wisp of smoke rising from the sea on the horizon. Turning himself once more into a hawk he flew swiftly towards the smoke and soon found himself above the sea hag's chimney.

Now he summoned up the form of the hedgehog and, curling himself into a prickly ball, he dropped down through the chimney and landed beside his lovely wife, who was busy making supper for her mistress. How

overjoyed she was when the hedgehog changed into Sean.

'Why did you come here, beloved husband?' said his wife. 'No man can get the better of the sea hag. She has nails of steel upon her fingers, as long as her hands, that would strip your flesh from head to heels.'

But Sean was not afraid even when the hag herself came in and flew at him with her nails. Quickly calling on the bear, he changed his form and seized the old hag round the waist, pressing hard until her backbone snapped and she lay dead.

That done, he turned into a man again and embraced his wife. 'Now we are safe,' he said, 'and we can leave this place. I shall take you home, back to my father's farm.'

And after changing them both to hawks, he flew with his wife to fair Kinsale. When they had retaken human form, Sean took her into the cottage to greet his parents and six brothers, who were overjoyed to see him: and he now a married grown-up lad.

Another feast was held that day and the next, and all the folk of Kinsale were invited to it. Sean and his wife settled down to work the land; and if Sean and his father were poor in times gone by, it's rich they were forever more.

Tom Thumb in Deventer

There was once an old farmer and his wife who lived at Deventer in the north of Holland. How they longed for a little child – a daughter or a son; but they had none.

Early one spring morning, Farmer Klaas went off to work as usual in his potato field, across the River Issel, while his wife Grietje set to making pancakes for his lunch. As she mixed the dough, she murmured sadly to herself, 'Oh how I wish I had a son. He could take these pancakes to his Dad!'

All of a sudden, there was a pop and a sizzle and a clip-clap-clop! And out of the mixture sprang a teeny-tiny boy, no taller than a thumb.

He stood before her on the table, wee arms resting on wee hips. 'Hello there, Mum,' he piped.

The poor woman stared. 'Well I never,' she cried. 'Where did you come from?'

And the tiny figure said, 'I popped out of the pancake mixture: clip-clap-clop! My name is Wee Tom Thumb.'

As her eyes grew wider in surprise, the cheeky voice went on, 'Come now, Mummy, don't stand there gawking. Make the pancakes for me to take to Dad.'

Dumbly, the farmer's wife tied five pancakes in a cloth and gave them to the tiny lad. Then, poking a stick through the bundle, Tom put the stick over his shoulder and strode off to the fields.

Just as he crossed the bridge – over by Bolwerk sawmill – oh dearie me! Poor Tom tripped and fell, splish-splash, into a ditch.

'Help, help! I'm drowning!' his shrill cries echoed across the field to where Farmer Klaas was hoeing.

Imagine the old man's surprise when he rushed towards the cries and found the tiny figure in the ditch. He could not believe his eyes.

'Don't stand there gaping, Dad,' Tom gurgled. 'Quick, help me out.'

In a daze, old Klaas bent down and lifted out the laddie, dripping wet, and gently set him down beside him.

'Where did you spring from?' Klaas said at last.

'Well, Dad, it's a tale as short as me: I popped out of the pancake mixture – clip-clap-clop. Here, I brought you some pancakes, though they're quite soggy now.'

As the old man sat down to eat, Tom Thumb piped up, 'Hold on here, Dad, I'll do some hoeing for you.'

'A little mite like you?' cried Klaas in disbelief. 'Why, you wouldn't have the strength.'

'Just watch me, then,' Tom said.

And he hopped up on the wooden hoe and set to work. All by himself. And as he hoed, he sang a song,

'One potato, two potato, three potato, four,
Five potato, six potato, seven potato, more.'

About that time, Squire Jansen was travelling along the Bolwerksweg in his carriage. He noticed the farmer sitting and munching pancakes, while his hoe worked on alone. Jansen halted his carriage right away and gave a puzzled shout, 'Hey, you there, why's your hoe hoeing by itself?'

'Ah now,' said Klaas with a smile, 'that's my boy working. That's him singing too.'

As he came closer, the squire heard the singing and

spotted Tom Thumb atop the wooden hoe. His eyes grew
as round as saucers, his ruddy face grew redder than a
beetroot. 'I'll buy him from you,' he said at once, reaching
for his gold. 'What's your price? Ten, twenty, fifty gilders?'

'No, no, I wouldn't dream . . .' began the farmer.

But Tom Thumb whispered in his ear, 'Go on, Dad, sell
me. Don't worry, I'll be back in two shakes of a donkey's
tail.'

So Farmer Klaas sold the mite for a hundred gilders.
And Squire Jansen counted out the coins, snatched up the
boy and wrapped him in his handkerchief. Thrusting it
into his pocket, he hurried home to tell his wife.

'Mistress, dearest, I've a big surprise for you,' he cried on
reaching home. And he began to rummage in his pockets.

'Well come on, you oaf, where is it then?' the Mistress
shouted impatiently.

Taking out his handkerchief, the squire unfolded it on
the tablecloth, and stood back amazed.

For it was empty!

Wee Tom Thumb had long since scampered home, back
to his Mum and Dad.

Some time later, one summer's evening, Tom Thumb
and his father were coming back from picking sugar beet.
Tom was riding on his father's wheelbarrow – which held a
load of sugar beet. When they came to the bridge across
the river, Tom sat on the very edge of the barrow, his legs
dangling down. He liked that because it gave him a bumpy
ride across the wooden bridge, so that when he tried to say
'oh' or 'ah', his voice wobbled like a croaking frog living in
the Wilpse dike. And if he said 'ee', it was just like the
cricket on the baker's hearth at Rishout.

He was enjoying himself so much that he forgot to hold
on to the barrow's edge and, as there was an extra big
bump at the end of the bridge, he toppled backwards right
into the tops of sugar beet.

Then, as the wheelbarrow trundled over the cobblestones of the Welle, he slid deeper and deeper into the
load and could not climb out at all. Although he shouted
hard, his father did not hear because of the coaches rattling
past. In any case, Klaas's thoughts were fixed on his old
sick cow at home. When they reached the cowshed, Klaas
tipped the load of sugar beet tops upon the ground for the

cow to eat and build up her strength.

By and by, as the farmer and his wife sat down to supper, Grietje looked up in alarm. 'Where is our little boy?' she said.

'Dear, oh dear,' cried Farmer Klaas. 'I quite forgot. I left him in the barrow.'

They rushed out-of-doors together. But the little fellow was nowhere to be seen: not in the yard, not in the cellar or the loft, not in the cowshed.

'Tom, Tom, Tom,' the woman shouted.

'Thumb, Thumb, Thumb,' the old man cried.

But there was neither sight nor sound of the little lad. Mother became afraid that Dad had lost him somewhere on the road, that he was gone for good. She got terribly upset and started crying, calling through her tears, 'Tom Thumb, my little son, where are you?'

All of a sudden they heard a teeny-weeny voice from far away. 'Here I am, quite safe and sound; inside the cow I can be found.'

The old pair wondered what to do. Mother wanted to kill the poor cow there and then. But Father would not have it.

Off he dashed to the chemist's for some castor oil and came back in a moment with an enormous bottle. He poured a big jugful of that down the poor cow's throat. Then Farmer Klaas and his wife stood back and waited while the good mixture did its work.

In no time at all the cow began to moo, lift her tail and drop first one pat, then a second and a third upon the ground. And then, as the tenth pat hit the earth, there was Tom Thumb, covered in muck from top to toe.

'Quick,' cried Mother, holding her nose. 'Under the pump with him.'

The smell, I might tell you, was simply awful.

Father pumped the handle up and down, dousing the tiny boy in cold water spray. Mother, meanwhile, grabbed a scrubbing brush and worked away at his clothes and hair. Presently, they took Tom indoors, undressed him and dropped him in a soapy bath; then they washed and scrubbed him once more as if it were a Sunday night. At last, there he sat upon the table as bright and clean as a brand new pin.

If you got very close, however, oh dear me, you could still tell where he'd been.

The Snow Queen

In the great Danish city of Copenhagen there once lived two poor children whose garden was no more than several flower pots. Though they were not brother and sister, they loved each other as much as if they had been; they lived in attics just across the way from one another. The street was so narrow that the rooftops on each side almost touched and you could step right across from one window to the other.

The boy's name was Kai, the girl was Gerda.

Each attic family had put a flower box upon the roof outside the window and filled it with rose bushes and cooking herbs. Sweet peas linked their long green runners from box to box and the rose bushes intertwined to make a flowery arch across the street. Thus, the two attics were connected by a little garden.

The flower boxes were quite tall, and the children knew they were not to climb across; but they were allowed to take their little stools and sit next to the arch. Thus passed many a delightful hour.

Winter brought an end to these delights: the windows were tightly shut to resist the cold. And when the panes frosted over, the children would heat a penny on the stove and hold it to the glass to melt the ice and form a little peep-hole; through these round holes would sparkle a little eye.

160

One day in winter Kai and Gerda were sitting together indoors looking at a picture book when suddenly – it was precisely five o'clock: the church tower clock had just struck the hour – Kai shouted out in pain, 'Oh, that hurts! Something pricked my chest.'

And then again, 'Ouch, something's in my eye!'

The little girl held his head still and inspected his eyes as he blinked hard, but there was nothing to be seen.

'I think it's gone now,' he murmured.

But it had not.

Truth to tell, he had been struck by two glass splinters from the Devil's Mirror. This was the work of a wicked magician who had made a Magic Mirror which he'd smashed into a million pieces; these now flew about the air, each one hardly bigger than a grain of sand. When a splinter entered people's eyes, it made them see things back to front: they saw only ugliness in beauty, and good in evil. Some poor souls were unlucky enough to receive a splinter in their heart, turning it in time to ice.

Poor Kai had these magic splinters in both heart and eye. His heart would shortly turn to ice and his eye would find fault with all it saw. Thenceforth he did not care whose feelings he was wounding; he even began to tease little Gerda who loved him dearly, and made her cry.

'Why are you blubbering?' he would shout. 'You look so ugly when you cry.'

'Look at that worm-eaten rose,' he shouted once. 'And look here at this one, how miserable it is. They're nasty, all of them, so's the box they're growing in.'

And he kicked the box and tore up the lovely roses. Then he ran away to play outside with the city boys.

The most daring of the city lads would tie their sleds to the farmers' carts and hitch a ride behind them; this they thought great fun. While they were playing that day a big white sledge drove by, bearing a person in a white fur coat with a white fur hat to match. The sledge drove twice around the square quite slowly and Kai hitched up behind it.

Off they went, faster and faster through the town. By now Kai was rather frightened and wanted to untie his sled, but each time he went to do so, the driver turned and nodded as if to reassure him. It was as if they were old friends.

So Kai sat still and they passed on through the city gates;

it was snowing so thickly that the boy could not see his hand before his face. He tried to undo the cord and free himself but it was no use. His little sled would not break loose. It was swept on as swiftly as the wind. Kai cried out as loudly as he could, but no one heard him. The snow fell thickly and the sledge flew fast. Every now and then it made a jump as if driving over a hedge or ditch. The boy was very frightened.

All at once the big sledge stopped and the driver turned to face him. And now he saw that the fur coat and hat were made entirely of snow. The driver was a woman: tall and slender and dazzlingly white, her eyes gleaming like two bright stars.

It was the Snow Queen!

163

'Are you cold?' she asked as she approached and kissed his brow. Her kiss was colder than a block of ice; the cold went right to his heart which was already all but frozen. He felt that he would die. Yet the feeling passed in a moment and he was no longer sensitive to the cold.

'Climb upon my sledge,' the Snow Queen said, 'and I will take you to see wonders beyond your wildest dreams.'

Kai looked at the Snow Queen. She was certainly very beautiful; a wiser and lovelier woman he could not imagine. Her eyes no longer appeared to him to be of ice: she was now so perfect that he felt no fear.

The Snow Queen smiled as he climbed into the sledge and suddenly Kai felt himself rising through the black clouds while a thunder storm was raging, out into moonlit skies. They flew together over lakes and forests, plains and oceans, while the North Wind whistled, the grey wolves howled, the white snow glittered and the black crows flew cawing over the trees. Above them shone the big round Moon, so clear and tranquil.

Thus Kai spent the long, cold winter night, while during the day he fell asleep at the Snow Queen's feet.

*   *   *

But what of little Gerda after Kai did not return? Where could he be, she wondered. No one knew. One boy said he had seen Kai tie his sled to a big white sledge that drove off through the city gates.

As time went by, people said he must be dead, no doubt drowned in the river beyond the town. Oh how long and dismal was the winter now!

Little Gerda cried and cried.

At last spring came to warm the land, but Kai had not returned.

'Kai must be dead,' moaned little Gerda.

'Indeed, that is not so,' the sunbeams breathed.

'He must be dead and gone,' she told the swallows.

'Indeed, that is not so,' they answered.

That gave her heart.

'I shall put on my new red shoes,' she said early one morning, 'the ones that Kai has never seen. And I'll go down to the river to ask about him.'

So she kissed her grandmother who was still sleeping, put on her new red shoes and went alone through the city gates and out towards the river.

'Is it true,' she asked the waves, 'that you have taken Kai away? I shall give you my red shoes if you will bring him back.'

She fancied the ripples of the river nodded strangely to her: so she took off her shoes – even though she prized them more than all else she owned – and threw them to the stream. They fell into the water just by the bank and the waves returned them to her, as if they would not take them. But little Gerda thought she had not thrown the shoes in far enough. Therefore, stepping into a little boat that lay among the reeds, she cast the shoes out into mid-stream. Suddenly, the boat, not being fastened, began to move, and little Gerda hastened to escape. It was too late. The boat was already too far from land. It picked up speed and swiftly floated with the current down the river.

Poor Gerda was very frightened and began to cry. But no one heard her save the little sparrows, and they could not take her back to land. To keep her company they flew along the banks, singing, 'Have no fear, Gerda, have no fear.'

Gerda sat very still. Her new red shoes floated on behind the boat, just out of reach. Gerda was now travelling past lovely countryside. Along the daisy-covered banks were stately trees, with green hills in the distance on which grazed sheep and cows. But not a single person came in sight.

'Perhaps the river will take me to dear Kai,' thought Gerda, and she cheered up at the thought.

At long last the boat drifted towards the river bank, near a little cottage with thatched roof and stained-glass windows. Before the door stood two toy soldiers who presented arms when they caught sight of the girl. Gerda called out to them, but they did not reply.

All at once an old lady leaning on a stick appeared at the open cottage door. She wore a large-brimmed hat adorned with every flower imaginable.

'Poor little child,' she said on seeing Gerda. 'The mighty river has brought you far from home.'

Thereupon she pulled the boat into the bank with her walking stick and led out the little girl. How glad Gerda was to be on dry land again. But she was a mite afraid of the strange tall lady.

'Come in and tell me who you are and how you came to

be here,' the woman said to Gerda.

When Gerda had told her all there was to tell, the old lady shook her head and clicked her tongue. And when Gerda asked if she had seen poor Kai, she said he had not passed but he was sure to come there soon.

'In the meantime, don't be sad,' she said. 'You can stay with me and eat ripe cherries, look at my flower garden which is prettier than any picture book; each flower can tell a different story.'

As Gerda gazed about the room she saw that the windows had panes of different coloured glass – of red and

blue and yellow, so that as the daylight filtered through, it lit up the room most splendidly in rainbow hues. Upon a table in the centre was a bowl of dark red cherries; Gerda could have as many as she liked. While she was eating, the old woman combed Gerda's hair with a golden comb, so that her flaxen ringlets curled about her lovely rosebud face.

'I've always wanted a little girl like you,' the lady said. 'I'm sure we'll get on well together.'

As her hair was being combed, Gerda's thoughts of her playmate Kai began to dim. For, in truth, the old woman was a sorceress. But not an evil one; she just liked to try a little magic now and then for her own amusement. And now she wanted very much to keep Gerda with her. Knowing that if the girl saw roses she would recall the roses at her home and then the lost boy Kai, she went into the garden and pointed her stick at every rose bush. Thereupon the full-leaved blossoms sank into the soil and vanished without trace. No one would have guessed that roses had once grown there.

'Let me show you my flower garden,' she said later, leading Gerda by the hand.

Oh, how beautiful and fragrant the garden was. Flowers of every country and season grew there in colourful abundance, all of them in full bloom. To be sure, no picture book could compare in beauty. Gerda clapped her hands for joy, and played among the flowers until the red sun set behind the cherry trees. Then she was given a pretty little bed with dark red pillows filled with violets; and there she slept so sweetly, dreaming rosier dreams than a queen before her coronation.

Next day she played again among the flowers, warmed by dancing sunbeams. Many days thus passed in happy playtime. Gerda soon knew every flower in the garden and, although there were more than she could count, it seemed that one kind was missing. She could not think which it was.

One afternoon, she was sitting with the lady and by chance looked at her wide-brimmed hat, the one adorned with all the flowers. The most beautiful amongst them was the rose – the old woman had quite forgotten the rose upon her hat when she'd hidden all the roses in her garden.

'That's the flower that's missing!' cried Gerda. 'There are no roses in the garden.'

And she ran to search among the flowers; but she did not find the rose. So sad was she that she sat and wept, and her teardrops fell upon the spot where a rose bush once grew. As soon as her warm tears touched the earth, the bush climbed up anew, as fresh and blooming as it ever was before. At once Gerda kissed the blossoms and thought of those at home and dearest Kai.

'Oh, how could I remain so long?' she cried. 'I must find little Kai. Do you know where he is?' she asked the roses. 'Do you think that he is dead?'

'No, he can't be dead,' the roses said, 'for we've been underground, where dead people are, and Kai wasn't there.'

'I thank you,' said little Gerda, and she went to ask the other flowers in turn if they knew where Kai was now.

But none could help her.

Finally, she fled as fast as she could to the garden gate, turned the rusty latch and pushed it open; she ran barefoot into the wide, wide world. Three times she glanced back to see if she was being followed. But no one came, so she ran on. When she could run no more she sank down upon a stone to rest. Casting a glance around she noticed in alarm that it was autumn in the outside world. Of course, in the enchanted garden, time stood still and it was always summer, with warm sunshine and full blooms.

'I've wasted so much time!' cried little Gerda. 'It is now late autumn; there's no time to lose.'

And off she ran again. But her little feet were bare and sore and all around her was so cold and barren. Droplets of autumn mist dripped down from the willow whose long yellow leaves were falling one by one. The hawthorn alone still bore a fruit, but its berries were so sharp and bitter. The world seemed cold and grey and sad that autumn day.

'How will I find Kai now?' she groaned aloud.

Suddenly she heard a cooing above her in the trees. It was a lone wood pigeon.

'I have seen your little friend. He was in the Snow Queen's chariot which passed above this wood while I was in my nest. The Snow Queen breathed on my young and killed them all; I alone survived – coo, coo, coo.'

'Where was the Snow Queen going, do you know?' asked the barefoot girl.

'She was travelling to Lapland where there's snow and ice the whole year round,' the pigeon said. 'Ask the

reindeer over there, he's bound to know the way.'

When Gerda approached him and told her tale, the reindeer said, 'It really is a glorious land, where you can run and play in quiet valleys, with snow and ice all through the year. It's there the Snow Queen has her summer tent, but her palace is a good way further, near the North Pole, on the island that men call Spitsbergen.'

'Poor Kai, dear Kai,' sighed Gerda.

'Climb upon my back. I'll take you if you like,' he offered.

Gerda clambered up and the reindeer bounded through the forest and across the plain; the wolves howled, the ravens shrieked and suddenly the sky was filled with shimmering coloured light.

'Those are the Northern Lights,' the reindeer said. 'See how beautiful they are.'

After some time they came to a little hut in the middle of a valley; it was the home of a wise old Lapp woman.

The reindeer related Gerda's story and in reply the Lapp woman told them, 'Kai is with the Snow Queen; in her palace everything is as he likes. He thinks it the best place in the world to be. That is because he has magic splinters in his heart and eyes. As long as they remain he will never become a boy again, and the Snow Queen will keep him in her power.'

'But can you not help Gerda to save the lad?' the reindeer said.

He pleaded so earnestly and Gerda had such tearful eyes

that the old Lapp woman spoke again, 'I can grant her no power as great as that she has already. Do you not realize how great it is? Do you not see how creatures help her on her way? How else could a little barefoot maid have come so far? Her power is more than ours because it comes from a loving heart. She is young and kind and would give her life to help another. Therein lies her power. If by herself she cannot reach the Snow Queen's palace and melt Kai's icy splinters, there is nothing we can do.'

So said the wise old woman of Lapland.

Off raced the reindeer once again, faster than the wind until at last, after many days and nights, he reached the icy gates of the Snow Queen's palace.

The walls of the palace were made of snowdrifts in which sharp winds had cut out windows and a door. It had over a hundred halls, many so long that it was not possible to see from one end to the other. All were lit up by the Northern Lights and all were empty, icy cold and dazzling white. No sounds of laughter resounded in those dreary chambers; no cheerful scene refreshed the heart.

In the centre of the main snow chamber was a frozen lake that had cracked into a thousand pieces like a vast mosaic. When at home, the Snow Queen always sat upon her throne of ice in the middle of the lake; she called it her Mirror of True Reason and declared it to be the wisest mirror in the world.

Meanwhile, little Kai was blue – no, almost black – with cold, though he did not notice, for the Snow Queen had kissed away the pain and turned his heart to ice. He was busy with the lake mosaic, joining together the icy pieces into varied patterns; the Snow Queen called this the Game of Reason and, in his eyes, the patterns were of the utmost beauty. He even formed entire words, but there was one word he could never spell:

ETERNITY.

The Snow Queen said that if he could form that word she would reward him with his freedom and a new pair of skates besides. Yet he could never do it.

'I am going now to warmer climes,' the Snow Queen said one morning. 'I shall take a look at my cooking pots (*by which she meant the volcanoes, Etna and Vesuvius*). I'll whiten them a little with frosty caps.'

So away she flew and Kai was left alone in the empty hall of ice. He sat pondering over the pieces of the lake, thinking and thinking until his poor head ached. He sat so stiff and still that one might have taken him for another block of ice.

It was at that moment that little Gerda passed through the palace gates, braving the icy winds that cut her to the bone, and entered the enormous hall.

She saw Kai at once and ran towards him, hugging him
tight and crying, 'Kai, dear Kai, I've found you at last, my
dear companion.'

But he sat still and cold, unfeeling, silent, stony-faced.
His lack of feeling wounded Gerda deeply and she burst
into bitter tears. Some of her warm teardrops fell upon his
breast, touched his heart and thawed the icy splinter.
Slowly he looked at her and tears came into his own eyes.
So hard did he cry that he washed away the icy splinter
there as well.

'Gerda, Gerda!' he cried with joy. 'Why have you been
so long?'

Kai looked about him. 'How cold it is! What am I doing
here?' he said.

And he embraced her whilst she laughed and wept by
turns. Even the icy pieces of the lake shared in their joy and

danced about, tinkling and jigging; when they were tired they lay down to form the letters of one word:

ETERNITY.

The very word the Snow Queen had said would gain Kai his freedom!

Gerda kissed his cheeks; they turned pink and glowing. She kissed his eyes; and they sparkled like her own. She kissed his hands and feet; and their colour flooded back. Kai soon became quite well and strong. Now the Snow Queen could come back just when she liked, it mattered not, for Kai's freedom was inscribed in icy letters on the floor.

They took each other by the hand and wandered from the palace, talking all the while about their lovely roses back at home. As they passed out through the palace gates the winds were hushed to calm and the Sun broke through the clouds. At the gates they found the reindeer standing by, awaiting their return; he had summoned another younger reindeer whose udder was full of milk. And she gladly gave her warm milk to refresh the young companions. Then the old buck and his hind carried the children back to the land where green leaves begin to sprout. There they made their farewells.

Soon the young pair heard the chirping of the first birds of spring and saw the greenwood in full bloom. Kai and Gerda walked on hand in hand, and wherever they went spring greeted them in all its splendour. Finally they arrived at Copenhagen and recognized the sound of bells from the church near their home.

With hearts beating fast they climbed the stairs to their familiar attic rooms: the clock greeted them as ever with its tick, tick, tick, and the hands moved onwards as before. The rose trees on the rooftop were in full bloom before the open window and there beneath them stood the little stools. Still hand in hand, Kai and Gerda sat down underneath the arch of roses. All memory of the Snow Queen's palace with its empty splendour was far behind.

Only one thing was now different.

For as they gazed fondly at each other they saw that they were now full grown, no longer children. And they were full content, while all around them blossomed the warm and glorious summer.

The Little White Duck

There was once a prince who married a fair princess. They barely had time to gaze on one another and exchange endearing words before the prince had to abandon his new wife and go off to war.

Of course, the princess wept and implored him not to go; but war is war. You cannot sit in peace embracing forever. And as was the custom when lords left their ladies in those times, the prince was forthright with his bride. She was not to go beyond the castle walls, nor to wander in the castle grounds, nor to gossip or harken to idle talk.

Dutifully, the princess vowed to do as she was told. And after the prince departed she awaited his longed-for return in solitude.

In the passing of time came an old woman, such a simple open soul.

'Why do you pine and grieve so?' she gently asked.

'Come, take a peep at God's clear light, walk about the gardens and breathe in the good fresh air.'

For a long time the princess resisted, yet finally gave way. 'No harm can come from walking in the gardens,' she thought to herself.

So out she went. And as she wandered through the castle grounds, a fountain of water, crystal clear, met her gaze.

'Well now,' said the old woman, 'the day is warm, the sun is high and the water cool; see how its spray glistens in the sun. Will you bathe?'

'No, no, I must not,' cried the princess. Yet next moment she was thinking to herself, 'Surely no harm will come from bathing in the water.'

So she slipped off her robe and slid into the fountain. No sooner had she done so than the old woman cackled cruelly, 'Fly, fly, Little White Duck!'

And the princess was turned into a duck flying round and round in the castle garden.

The wicked witch – for that is what the old crone was – now donned the royal robe, assumed the form of the princess (so that none could have told the two apart) and seated herself in the castle tower to await the prince.

175

Not long after, the hounds began to yelp, the bells to toll, and the royal carriage returned. The witch-princess rushed to greet her noble lord, threw her arms about his neck, kissed and flattered him. And he, unsuspecting, held her in his arms, never thinking that she was not what she appeared to be.

Meanwhile, in a quiet corner of the castle grounds, the Little White Duck laid three eggs and from them hatched three human children: two strong and handsome boys and an ugly puny girl. The mother raised them, taught them how to swim, catch goldfish, gather leaves and bark and sew themselves some winter clothes. Although she warned them not to stray too far, sometimes they disobeyed her, for they were fond of playing in the soft green grass beneath the castle windows.

One day when they were four or five years old, the nose of the witch-princess began to twitch as she caught their scent and straightaway knew them for who they were. She ground her teeth in anger; yet she called them inside to her, fed and pampered them. Then, when they had tired themselves in play, she prepared a bed for them to sleep. And as soon as they were tucked up snug and warm, she bade the servants kindle a great fire, put cauldrons of water to heat upon the flames and sharpen up some knives.

In the meantime, the two brothers fell asleep, but their

sister watched and listened to all that passed. Deep in the night the witch-princess came to their door and whispered, 'Are you awake, little ones, are you awake?'

And the ugly puny sister answered,

> 'We cannot sleep, we sit and weep,
> For knowing thee, you'll slay us three.
> Purple the fire for our funeral pyre,
> Sharp the knife to end our life.'

The witch went away, walked up and down impatiently, then by and by returned. 'Are you awake, little ones, are you awake?' she called.

And again the little sister answered for her brothers,

> 'We cannot sleep, we sit and weep,
> For knowing thee, you'll slay us three.
> Purple the fire for our funeral pyre,
> Sharp the knife to end our life.'

'The very same answer in a single voice!' muttered the witch. 'I'd better make sure they're all awake.'

Quietly she opened the door and, seeing both brothers sound asleep, she burst into the room and quickly smothered all three children.

Next morning, when the Little White Duck called her children to her, no one came. With deep foreboding she spread her wings and flew into the castle courtyard. And there, white as a sheet, cold as sleet, lay her three children in a row upon the cobblestones. The poor mother threw herself upon her dead children, covering their little bodies with her wings and crying,

'Quack, quack, my little loves,
Quack, quack, my turtledoves,
I cared for you in tender years,
Washed you daily in my tears,
Kept watch throughout the long dark night
And never let you out of sight.'

From inside the castle the prince happened to hear the sad complaint of the mother duck and called to the witch-princess, 'Wife, did you ever hear the like: a duck talking in a human voice?'

But the evil witch replied, 'It's just your fancy, sire.' And, calling to the servants, she cried, 'Drive that wretched bird out of the courtyard.'

Although the men dashed this way and that, they could not catch the duck, for she flew round and round above their heads making them stumble and knock each other down. Ever again she returned to the still white forms of the little children, crying,

'Quack, quack, my little loves,
Quack, quack, my turtledoves,
I cared for you in tender years,
Washed you daily in my tears,
Kept watch throughout the long dark night
And never let you out of sight.'

And then to the astonishment of all she sang a new song,

'The witch took away your father fine,
The royal prince, dear husband mine.
She cast me in the castle spring,
And crowned herself the royal queen.'

As the prince heard these words, he knew he had been deceived. 'Hey there, servants,' he shouted from his window, 'catch that duck and bring it to me.'

Flunkeys and footmen set to trap the bird, but try as they might they just succeeded in tripping each other up again. Only when the prince himself came into the courtyard did the Little White Duck fly instantly to his hands. And as he stroked her feathered wings the duck became a lovely maiden whom he knew at once as his own dear wife.

Immediately she summoned a magpie who was sent to fetch two phials of water: the Water of Life and the Water of Speech. When the bird returned, the princess sprinkled a few drops of the Water of Life over her three children . . . And their cold white bodies stirred to life.

Then she sprinkled the Water of Speech over their heads . . . And their numbed lips slowly moved and happy cries rose from them.

Now at last with their dear family about them the prince and princess began to live in peace and prosperity.

As for the witch, she was tied to the tail of a wild stallion and dragged away across the plain. Where a leg came off, a black poker stood; where an arm snapped free, a rake now stood; where her head fell off, a wild bramble grew. Then down swooped the crows to peck at her flesh, and up swept the winds to scatter her bones.

And not a scrap, not a trace or a speck was left of the wicked witch.

The Golden Goose

Long ago, in Germany, there was a couple who had three sons. The two eldest lads were bright and wise, but the youngest – oh dearie me – was nicknamed Blockhead for his silly ways.

One day, as the eldest son was in the forest cutting wood, a little old man approached, then stopped to stare. When lunchtime came, the lad sat down to refresh himself from the pie and wine his mother had given him.

Up spoke the old man at last, 'Good day, young sir. I wonder, could you see your way to sparing a little wine and pie; I'm fair starving for lack of food.'

But the clever fellow said, 'Give you some wine and pie! I should think not. I've scarcely enough here for myself.'

At that the little old man snorted and left.

Some time later, when the son was completely refreshed, he set to work chopping down a tree. But his axe missed the trunk and cut his leg, forcing him to limp off home to have it dressed.

Next day the second son went to the forest for wood. He too was met by the little old man who begged for food and drink. But he was far too wise to share his lunch.

'Be off with you,' he cried. 'This wine and pie are for me.'

The old man clicked his tongue and went away.

By and by, as the second fellow set to work, his sharp axe slipped and cut his leg, making him stagger home.

It was the old man's revenge.

Next day, Blockhead said, 'Father, let me go for firewood.'

That made his father cross. 'Your brothers have lamed themselves,' he cried. 'What a dolt like you would do I hate to think! You stay at home.'

But Blockhead kept on so much that his father lost patience with him finally. 'Oh, go on then,' he said. 'Perhaps the axe will teach you a lesson too.'

All his mother gave him was dry black bread and a bottle of sour beer; and with this he went on his way. Once in the forest he set to work and cut up a pile of logs. Then at noontime, when the Sun was overhead, he sat down to rest with the lunch-bag upon his knees.

Just then the little old man appeared. 'Good day, young sir,' he began. 'I wonder, could you see your way to sparing a little bite to eat?'

'There's only dry black bread and sour beer,' the lad replied. 'But sit down and welcome, if you please.'

As the old man thanked him, the lad pulled out his bread and found it changed into a hot meat pie; and when he put the bottle to his lips, it had become cool white wine. So the two men ate and drank their fill.

When the meal was over the old man said, 'You've a kind heart, my lad; you deserve reward. Cut down that oak tree and look within.' With that he smiled and disappeared.

Blockhead took up his axe and cut down the tree. Lo and behold, he found in the roots a golden goose alive and

shining! Picking it up he wondered to himself: should he take it home or seek fortune in the world? The answer was plain. With the golden goose he need not suffer the taunts and bullying of his brothers. So off he marched towards the nearest inn, where he called for a bed and a place by the fire for his golden goose.

Now the landlord of that inn had three young daughters who were the most inquisitive girls; and when they set eyes on the golden goose they wished to pluck a feather each from its gleaming tail. So as soon as Blockhead had gone to bed, the eldest crept up to the sleeping goose and seized its tail to pull a feather. But to her surprise, her fingers were stuck: however hard she pulled she could not free her hand. And when her sister tried to help, she stuck fast to the first one's waist. At that, the youngest maid tugged and pulled on the second's dress, but stuck as fast as the previous two. The three had to stay with the goose all night.

At dawn next day the young man rose and picked up his golden goose; he cast not a glance at the unfortunate girls as he sauntered down the lane. Wherever he went the sisters followed, like it or not, fast or slow.

As they passed a church later that day, they were hailed from the window by a parson dressed in black. He wagged his finger and clucked his tongue, 'Girls, how dare you pursue a young man like that! Let go of him at once.'

He ran out and seized the youngest by her wrist. But the moment he touched her his hand stuck fast, and he trailed behind her, running to keep up.

Presently the churchwarden, a stout little man, was shocked to see such a sight: the tall thin parson pursuing young girls; whatever would the parish think!

And he ran and clutched at the parson's cloak. He too stuck fast.

So now there were five, all in a line, tripping and stumbling after the lad. He did not mind: he whistled and sang as he carried the goose on his arm. Along the way they met two farmers in a field, one with a rake and one with a hoe.

'Hey there, good men,' the parson cried, 'for God's sake lend us a hand.'

They did as he said. Yet as they laid hands on the churchwarden's belt, they were pulled along in his wake. Now there were seven – what a funny sight – stepping on each other's heels, trailing behind the lad and his goose.

During the day they arrived at a town with a palace and a grieving king. The king, poor man, had an only child with a face as glum as can be. No one could make her laugh. So the king made it known to all of the world that any man who made her smile could wed the princess and take half the kingdom besides.

When Blockhead heard this, he went straight to the forlorn princess to show her his funny followers. The princess stared hard at the nine stuck fast:

> The lad and the goose,
> The three inn maids,
> The tall thin parson,
> The short fat warden,
> And the red-faced farmers,

All stumbling over each other's heels.
And she burst out laughing.
She could not help herself. Thus, the lad claimed his wife. As for the goose, he flew away, freeing the others.
So the fool became prince and later king, with a beautiful wife at his side. And he lived at ease for the rest of his days with nine happy children besides.

The Aztec Sun

Before the Sun that now shines brightly over Mexico came into being, there had been other suns; four in all. Each died away in turn before our present Sun appeared.

The fourth Sun, Chalchuitlicu, had been a water goddess, copper-coloured and dressed in emerald green. For hundreds of years she provided light and warmth; and in that time the first men and women appeared on Earth. But other gods grew jealous of the Sun God; some reproached her for giving fire to humans – for they did not always use it wisely.

One night, the black God of Darkness, Tezcatlipoca, began to torment the gentle copper Sun while she was resting in the gloom. He said she'd grown too vain and selfish. In her hurt at these false words, Chalchuitlicu burst into tears and lost control of the waters thus released. The tears put out her light and then the sky rained down upon the Earth in torrents.

The land vanished into darkness beneath a mighty flood which drowned all human life: every man and woman

turned into fish; all, that is, save one lone family which survived to start the human race again.

When the sky thus fell on Earth, the gods opened up four roads beneath the land, where they created four giants and some sturdy trees. And then, together – the gods, the trees, the giants – all tried to lift the Earth from under the vales of tears. They heaved and pushed until the land rose upwards and the waters fell away. At last they managed to fasten the land securely to the sky.

But the Earth was still plunged in utter gloom; it had no dawn, no dusk, no sunlit days. The vales of tears were salty: there was thus no fresh water, for no Sun appeared to draw the tears back up to heaven and change them into rain.

It was then that the gods resolved to give the world a fifth and final Sun. They assembled at Tectihuacan, Place-of-the-Gods, and argued loud and long. Eventually, it was decreed: There had to be a Sun.

And there must be moonlight while the Sun was at its rest.

But who would do the job?

After all, the first four suns had died away. The gods ordained a sacrifice: whoever volunteered would not live to see themselves as Sun or Moon, but would have to change their form so that the Sun and Moon could last forever.

Only one god came forward: Tecuciztecatl, God of Snails and Worms. He was rich and strong and vain. He thought by sacrificing himself he would gain immortal glory. He wished therefore to be the Sun.

No one else was willing. Uneasily the gods looked about them; there had to be a second sacrifice to make the Sun and the Moon. Their gaze fell at last upon a humble goddess in their midst: Little Nana, the unsightly one. If she agreed, the gods declared, they would transform her body.

Poor Nana did not want to die. Yet she smiled gently when they told her she might light up and warm the Earth; for she might help little children not yet born.

The gods began their preparations. Two tall stone altars were erected: one for the Sun, one for the Moon – though which was which had yet to be agreed. Both sacrifices were bathed and dressed in their own way.

The God of Snails and Worms put on a fine plumage

and brightly-coloured robes, ear-rings of turquoise and jade, and a collar of shining gold.

Little Nana had no such finery. So she daubed her red-raw body white and donned a thin, torn paper dress through which her puny body showed.

Meanwhile, beneath the altars, the gods had built a sacrificial pyre. So many logs of wood were heaped upon it that the heavens seemed to light up in the roaring blaze. At this sight, the God of Snails trembled in fear and bit his lip; yet Little Nana sat quietly by, her hands folded in her lap.

Tecuciztecatl was honoured to be first to leap into the flames. At the gods' command, he drew near the pyre and stood tall and grand upon his pillar of white stone, his plume of red and green and yellow streaming in the breeze. But his courage failed him and he drew back abruptly, pale and trembling. Three times he was summoned, and three times he nervously stepped back.

The gods finally lost patience and turned to Little Nana, crying, 'Jump!'

She stepped forward instantly and stood unflinching on the pillar's edge. Then she closed her eyes, smiled bravely as she thought of her sacrifice for the people, and leapt into the red heart of the flames.

Angry and ashamed – but more afraid the noble power of the Sun would not be his – the God of Snails and Worms shut tight his eyes and jumped. But his leap was to one side, where the fire was weakest and the ash was thick.

Just then an eagle swooped from nowhere into the flames, then out again so quickly only his wingtips were singed. He flew upwards swiftly with a bright ball of fire held in his beak – like a fiery arrow through the sky – until he reached the eastern gates of Tectihuacan. There he left the ball of fire – for thus Little Nana had become – and she took her seat upon a throne of billowing clouds. She had golden shining tresses strung with pearls and precious shells, shimmering in the mists of dawn; her lips were brightest scarlet.

Never was the dawn so beautiful. A great roar of pleasure issued from the gods and rumbled through the morning sky.

And then a hawk swooped into the burning embers of the fire and was scorched a charcoal black; it emerged at once with a glowing, ash-coloured ball of fire held in its beak. And this it carried to the sky and placed beside the Sun.

Thus the cowardly God of Snails became the Moon.

The gods were angry with the feeble Moon and one flung a rabbit at him – the nearest thing at hand. The rabbit flew straight and true, striking the Moon full in the face. Ever since, when the Moon is full, you may see the scars left by the rabbit's long ears and flying feet.

As the Sun makes her journey around the world, bringing warmth and light, the Moon sets off in vain pursuit. But he is always slow to start; and when, cold and weary, he reaches the west, the Sun has long since set; by now his once-fine robes have turned to tatters.

That is the story of the fifth and final Sun.

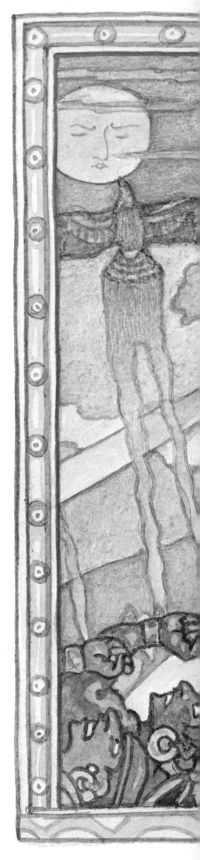

Peer Gynt

There once dwelt in Gudbrandsdale in the mountains of Norway a young man named Peer Gynt. He lived with his mother Aase in a tumbledown farm alongside a rushing mountain stream. Since his father's death, Peer had had to run the farm alone. But, alas, he'd let it go to ruin; for he was a lazy, good-for-nothing rascal whom his poor mother was forever scolding about his idle ways.

So it happened one summer's day: Peer had gone off for several weeks just when he was needed most; and now, on his return, Aase lashed him soundly with her tongue.

'You ragamuffin! You run off to the hills when you should be working in the fields. And now, here you are, your clothes are in tatters and you've lost your gun. What have you to say?'

'Well, Mother . . . it's like this,' said Peer mysteriously.

And he launched into one of his rambling stories: how he had seen a giant reindeer up in the snowclad hills, how he had shot it and sat astride the beast to skin it when – mercy on us – the buck had suddenly come to life and dashed off like lightning, Peer clinging to its neck. Over misty crags and brooding lakes, then through clouds into a land of trolls . . .

'Finally,' he said, 'we plunged into a mountain stream, spraying foam far around. I managed to escape, half-drowned, and scramble to the northern shore. And here I am, Mother, lucky to be alive.'

His mother stood and stared, wide-eyed; then she boxed his ears: for she had heard the tale before.

'You dress up your fibs in their Sunday best,' she complained, 'building castles in the air, lying left and right, you shameless scoundrel. It's all because of you that we are so poor and wretched.'

'Give me time,' exclaimed Peer cheerfully. 'I'll wed a princess one day and we'll live like royalty.'

'Who would have a tramp like you?' his mother scoffed. 'You could have married that girl at Heggstad if you'd gone about it right. Her father's made of money. But while you were riding reindeer through the sky, Mads Moen

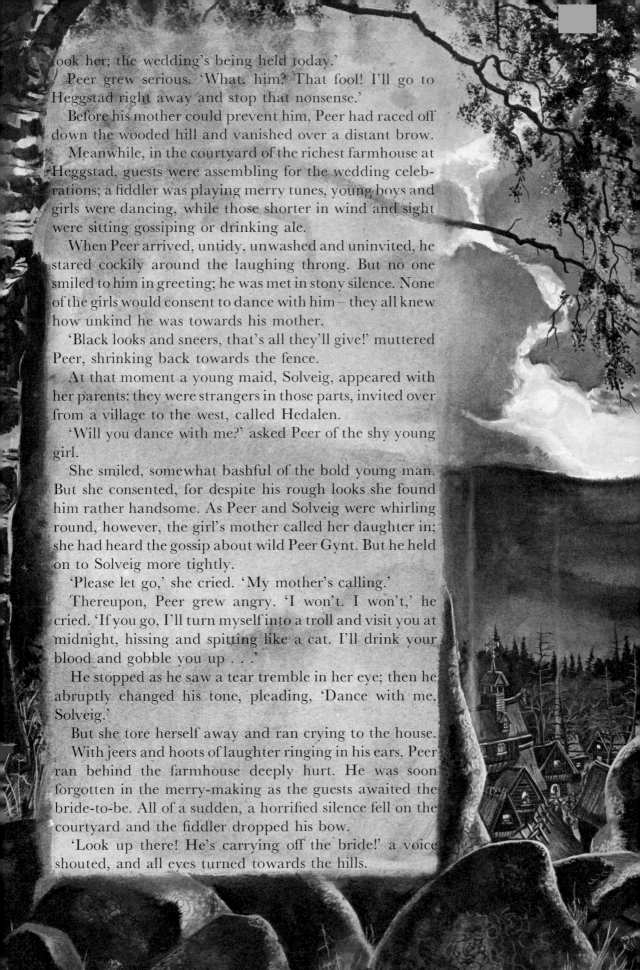

look her; the wedding's being held today.'

Peer grew serious. 'What, him? That fool! I'll go to Heggstad right away and stop that nonsense.'

Before his mother could prevent him, Peer had raced off down the wooded hill and vanished over a distant brow.

Meanwhile, in the courtyard of the richest farmhouse at Heggstad, guests were assembling for the wedding celebrations; a fiddler was playing merry tunes, young boys and girls were dancing, while those shorter in wind and sight were sitting gossiping or drinking ale.

When Peer arrived, untidy, unwashed and uninvited, he stared cockily around the laughing throng. But no one smiled to him in greeting; he was met in stony silence. None of the girls would consent to dance with him – they all knew how unkind he was towards his mother.

'Black looks and sneers, that's all they'll give!' muttered Peer, shrinking back towards the fence.

At that moment a young maid, Solveig, appeared with her parents: they were strangers in those parts, invited over from a village to the west, called Hedalen.

'Will you dance with me?' asked Peer of the shy young girl.

She smiled, somewhat bashful of the bold young man. But she consented, for despite his rough looks she found him rather handsome. As Peer and Solveig were whirling round, however, the girl's mother called her daughter in; she had heard the gossip about wild Peer Gynt. But he held on to Solveig more tightly.

'Please let go,' she cried. 'My mother's calling.'

Thereupon, Peer grew angry. 'I won't. I won't,' he cried. 'If you go, I'll turn myself into a troll and visit you at midnight, hissing and spitting like a cat. I'll drink your blood and gobble you up . . .'

He stopped as he saw a tear tremble in her eye; then he abruptly changed his tone, pleading, 'Dance with me, Solveig.'

But she tore herself away and ran crying to the house.

With jeers and hoots of laughter ringing in his ears, Peer ran behind the farmhouse deeply hurt. He was soon forgotten in the merry-making as the guests awaited the bride-to-be. All of a sudden, a horrified silence fell on the courtyard and the fiddler dropped his bow.

'Look up there! He's carrying off the bride!' a voice shouted, and all eyes turned towards the hills.

They saw Peer Gynt scrambling up the hillside like a
goat, dragging the weeping, white-clad bride behind him.
In a moment, the two had vanished into the trees.

'That scoundrel's ruined the wedding,' roared the poor
bride's father, white with fury. 'As God's my witness, I'll
hunt him down and strike him dead.'

In no time at all, all the guests had armed themselves
with clubs and guns and set off in pursuit, the bride's father
at their head.

In the meantime, once out of sight, Peer stole a kiss from
the tearful bride and left her to be rescued, giving a cheery
wave as he ran off, shouting back, 'The devil take all
women . . .'

And then he added, as he thought of Solveig, 'Excepting
one.'

With that he was gone, flinging his arms about and
leaping in the air like a madman.

'I can swim rapids and pull up fir-trees like a bear,' he
sang. 'I'll overturn the world. Peer Gynt, you're the
greatest. You'll be a prince before long.'

Just then he tripped, bumped his nose against a rock and
lay senseless on the ground.

When he awoke he found himself on a mountain slope
thick with giant firs and pines through which the wind was
howling. Stars were twinkling in the evening sky as Peer
shook himself and started to rise. All at once he caught his
breath: for there before him was a maid in green.

'Who are you?' he asked amazed; he had never set eyes on such a strange-looking girl.

'I am the daughter of King Brose of Dovre,' she replied.

'Oh, are you now?' he said smiling. 'And I'm the son of Queen Aase of Gudbrandsdale – Prince Peer. Where is your home?'

'I live in the palace of the Mountain King,' she said.

'Perhaps she speaks the truth,' mused Peer. 'I've always wished to wed a real princess. Now's my chance.'

'Do you like my silken robes and fur cloak?' the maiden asked, catching his eyes upon her clothes.

'They look more like tow and mouldy sacks to me,' he snorted.

'Ah, that's because you have no gift of second sight,' she said. 'With us evil's good and black is white; big is little and dull looks bright. You'd likely say my father's hall is a pile of rock; though, in truth, it is a shining palace. Would you like to see it, Prince Peer?'

Peer would like nothing better; in any case, he'd nowhere else to go. She gave a shout and, to his surprise, a giant rosy pig came trotting over the hillside. Taking the pig's rope bridle in her hands, the girl in green stepped into the saddle, bidding Peer sit behind her.

'Gee-up, gee-up, my trusty steed,' she cried.

The two trotted off into the dark of night seated upon the pig.

By and by, Peer and the maid in green entered a deep cave in the hillside and followed a track on foot down into the mountain until, at last, they came to a well-lit hall. Peer stared about him in amazement: hundreds of ugly, tail-swinging trolls of every shape and size were making merry: dancing, singing, drinking. At the far end of the hall sat the Mountain King upon his throne; his daughter was now whispering in his ear.

No sooner had the trolls set eyes on the human than they crowded round, shrieking with glee.

'Let me slice his fingers into shreds,' piped up a tiny troll.

'Let me take a big bite from his rump,' yelled a fat troll maiden.

'Shall we have him mashed up in porridge or minced in stew?' screamed a troll witch, brandishing a spoon.

'Wait!' came the king's roar. 'Our affairs have gone downhill of late. We could do with a rich prince to set us right. If I marry my daughter to this ugly brute he'd be sure to help us out.'

Turning to Peer, he said, 'So you wish to wed my daughter?'

'I never said so,' replied Peer. 'But since you ask I'll take her if you like – and your kingdom too as dowry.'

'I'll grant you half my kingdom now,' the Troll King said, 'the rest you'll get on the day I die. But you must pass the test of the trolls. Should you fail, you won't leave here alive. First you must close your mind to the outside world, the sunlit day, the starry night.'

'If I'm to be king that should make it easy,' Peer answered with a grin.

'Next you must wear a tail like one of us,' the king continued.

Peer did not take to this at all; but the king was firm.

'You can't wed my daughter with a bare backside,' he cried. 'Anyway, a tail is our mark of high esteem.'

'If I must, I must then, to be king,' Peer sighed.

When the tail was fixed, he wagged and whisked it about in style.

'Is there anything else I've got to do?' he asked.

The king waved a hand and two trolls with pigs' heads brought in food and drink.

'Our cows give cakes and our pigs give mead,' the king explained. 'You will have to get used to our homely fare.'

Peer pushed the bowls away; they smelt foul and putrid.

'Remember, Prince Peer,' the Troll King warned, 'whoever takes the bowl takes my daughter too.'

Peer swallowed hard, pinched his nose and mumbled to himself, 'No doubt I'll grow accustomed to the taste in time. Well, here goes . . .'

He drank the pig-made mead, but spat it out at once, pulling a horrid face. The troll courtiers laughed.

'Now we'll give our eyes and ears a treat,' King Brose cried. 'Harpist: pluck softly on your harp-strings. Dancer: step lightly upon the floor.'

At his command music and dancing commenced. After a while, the king asked Peer whether he enjoyed the concert; and he, unthinking, blurted out, 'What a racket! Fancy a cow in knickerbockers scraping her horns and a sow in stockings prancing round!'

The trolls all stared aghast.

'Let's lop off his ears, let's scratch out his eyes,' troll maidens cried.

The maid in green, Peer's bride-to-be, began to weep. 'How can you be so cruel when I and my sister play so well?' she sobbed.

'Was that you?' he cried astonished. 'I was only teasing.'

But the trolls would not forgive the insult to the royal pair.

'It's a strange thing, this human nature,' the Troll King mused. 'It sticks to a man like a fold of skin. My future son has willingly drunk our bowl of mead and fastened on a tail; I thought I'd chased away the man in him for good. But no. I must perform one final act to cure his human ills.'

The king waved his hand once more and sharp knives were carried in at once.

'Now, my son,' the king began, 'I shall cut out your eyes so that nothing will seem ugly to you.'

Peer drew back in horror, his hands held to his eyes. 'There's a limit to being king,' he muttered nervously. 'I'll wear a tail; I'll even swear a cow's a girl, and a sow's a princess, if you like. But I won't give up my eyes. You must be mad!'

'It's the king's decision, Prince Peer,' intoned an older troll. 'He is the wise one; it's you who's mad.'

'Let me out of here,' yelled Peer. 'I'm not a prince; nor am I rich. I made that up.'

The king glared at him in anger, then declared, 'Dash him to bits upon the rocks.'

At that a dozen shrill troll voices clamoured loudly, 'May we not torment him first, Your Majesty?'

The king nodded wearily and went to bed. Peer meanwhile rushed in panic through the hall chased by the shrieking trolls. 'Clear off, you devils,' he shouted, climbing up the chimney.

They pulled him down, biting his bottom and tearing out his hair.

'Ouch! Oh! Stop it!' shrieked Peer, trying to escape now through a trapdoor to the cellar.

'Shut all the exits,' yelled the younger imps.

Their elders smiled: 'They are so enjoying themselves, the little devils,' they said.

Peer was now fighting off a tiny troll which was clinging to his ear. 'Let go, you maggot,' he shouted out.

And off he rushed again, a host of ugly trolls in fierce pursuit. Suddenly, he fell full-length and the trolls pounced on him in a heap, pinning him to the ground.

'We've got him now,' they screamed in triumph.

'Skin him alive!'

Above the hubbub came the feeble cries of poor Peer Gynt, buried beneath a pile of trolls. 'Mother, help, help, they're killing me . . .'

All of a sudden, there came the distant tolling of church bells. As if by magic, the imps released their victim and, amid wild shrieks, they all fled in uproar from the hall.

Peer could scarcely believe that he was still alive. 'Whoever could have rung the bell and saved me?' he wondered, limping out into the cool night air.

He stumbled over clump and tussock, pitching and rolling down the hills, until he came in the dead of night to the parish church at Heggstad. And there, to his amazement, he discovered Solveig, ringing the church bell with all her might.

'I heard there were trolls in the mountains and I feared for you,' she shyly said. 'But you must not linger here, for the whole village is chasing you.'

Peer was deeply touched by the pure-hearted maiden who had saved his life. 'Come with me, Solveig,' he begged her. 'I'll build us a hut in the forest far away where we can live together; I'll take good care of you and even give up my wild ways.'

Thinking fondly of her parents, the girl shook her head in sorrowful silence. So Peer set out alone to build a hut of pinewood in the snow-clad forest high above the valley, hidden from folk's view. There he lived on elk-meat, berries and water from the melted snow. One day, at dusk, as Peer was standing in the doorway of his hut, fixing on a strong wooden bolt to secure his home against the trolls, he saw a figure slowly climbing the snow-covered hill on skis. It was a woman in a grey shawl carrying a little bundle.

'Solveig!' cried Peer. 'No, it can't be . . . Yes, it is. Why have you come?'

'A call came to me on the wind, a summons in my dreams, a cry in your dying mother's voice. The long, long nights and empty days told me that I must come. And when folk asked me where I was bound, I answered: "home".'

Peer wept in guilt and sadness at his mother's death – yet at the same time with joy at Solveig's coming. 'Let me look at you, Solveig; you are so pure and kind,' he said, tears glistening in his eyes. 'Let me carry you across the threshold, you are so warm and light. My wooden home, I fear, is not worthy of you.'

'I love it here,' said Solveig. 'I can breathe more freely; the valley was so stifling. I felt entombed. I can hear the sighing of the pines – silence and song together. Now I am truly at home.'

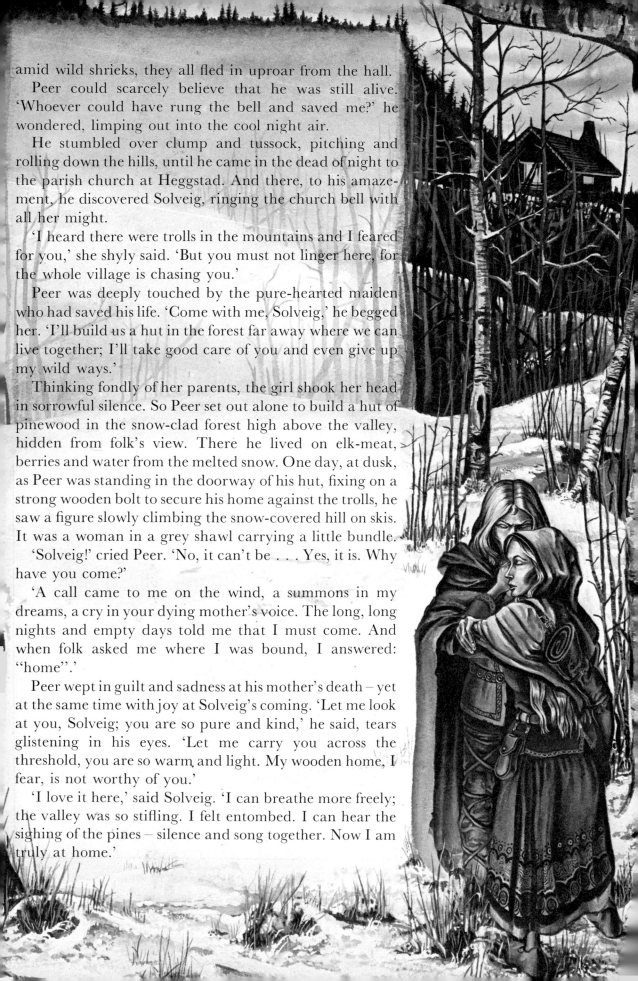

'Then come inside,' cried Peer, happier than he'd ever been before. 'I'll fetch some logs and light a fire.'

As Solveig entered, Peer closed the door and skipped joyfully towards the trees.

'At last, my dream princess has come,' he sang. 'I'll build a palace fit for her to live in.'

Taking up his axe, he began to swing it to and fro, chopping down a tree for firewood. As he gaily set about his work, however, a shadow fell across his path.

'Good evening to you, Prince Peer Gynt,' said a voice.

Looking up, he saw an ugly hag in a torn green smock.

'Who are you?' he asked alarmed.

'Why, Peer Gynt, we're neighbours,' she said. 'As you built your hut, so mine rose at its side.'

Peer was silent. There was something about the witch that was familiar. Uneasily, he picked up his logs and turned to go.

'Pardon me, I'm in a hurry,' he excused himself.

'You always were,' she said. 'Have you forgotten your promise to wed me? The tail, the bowl of mead, the pledges . . . Do you remember now?'

Peer recoiled in horror from the old green witch.

'Leave me in peace, you evil troll,' he shouted, 'or I'll brain you with my axe.'

'Oh no, Peer Gynt,' she smiled. 'That won't help you. I'll come back each day; I'll scratch out your bride's blue eyes – when her fair looks are gone, my own will return.'

With that she went off cackling into the undergrowth, leaving Peer in dumb despair.

'My palace has tumbled down before it's built,' he sighed, holding his head with trembling hands. 'Clearly happiness is not so easy to attain. First I must be cleansed of my unworthy past before deserving Solveig's love. And I must protect her from the trolls: she is in danger.'

'Are you coming, Peer?' called Solveig from the hut.

'I shall be a while yet. I have a heavy load to bear,' he replied.

'Then let me help,' she cried.

'No, I'll manage by myself,' he called. 'Be patient, dear Solveig, I may be gone some time.'

'I shall wait,' was all she said. Solveig remained in the open doorway, watching Peer disappear into the trees.

Time passed. Peer did not return that day or the next;

that year or the year to come. Ten, twenty, thirty years
went by and Solveig waited on for his return. Her home
remained the lonely hut up on the hill; she spent her days
tending goats and spinning wool. And she would often
gaze forlornly down the empty slope.

Where was Peer in all those years? What adventures did
he have? Alas, there were too many to relate. He was even
crowned king. His old dream had come true.

Yet he tired of his empty life and, as he grew old, he
thought more and more of Solveig and his hut upon the
wooded hills of Norway. So one day he set sail for home.

As the ship approached his native coast a fierce storm
blew up, overturned the vessel and sent his fortune to the
bottom of the sea. Peer was lucky to escape alive.

Looking like a beggar, he wandered through the mists of
the once-familiar land. Finally, in deep despair, he came to
a heather slope with a path winding upwards into the trees.

'I'll climb to the top of that misty peak,' he wheezed,
'and see the Sun rise one last time upon my native land.
Then, let the snow pile over my worthless shell and bury
me in its tomb. "Here Lies a Nobody" will be my epitaph.
"He has trod this Earth and left no Mark".'

Peer thought he heard a woman's song coming from
beyond the ridge. Once more he staggered on and suddenly
spied a wooden hut. In the doorway sat a white-haired
woman, with blind but gentle eyes. He recognized her at
once.

'Solveig!' he shouted, choking back his sobs.

The blind woman raised her head and started up,
groping down the path towards the shout.

'It's Peer. It's Peer,' she cried. 'He's come at last.'

Finding Peer, she sat down by his side, taking his head
upon her lap. They remained together for some time, silent
save for sobs that trembled in the air.

'May I ask you something?' Peer spoke at last. 'Do you
know where I have been since you saw me last?'

'That's easy,' whispered Solveig; 'you've been here
beside me all the time: in my faith, my hope, my love.'

Peer hid his face, moistened with tears, into her gentle
hands. And as he breathed his last faint breath, she softly
murmured, 'Your journey's over, Peer. At last you came
upon the truth of life: the greatest happiness lies right here
at home, not in chasing dreams about the world.'

Dorani

Once upon a time in Hindustan there lived a perfume seller who had a lovely daughter named Dorani. This maiden could sing and dance so beautifully that she was chosen to appear before Indira, the Queen of Fairyland. And the queen rewarded her with the most glorious hair in all the world.

So lovely was Dorani's coal-black hair that it shone like burnished ebony and had the fragrance of roses in full bloom. One day, for amusement, she cut off a lock of her hair, wrapped it in a broad magnolia leaf and cast it to the stream that flowed beneath her window.

The leaf floated on and on until it passed close by a prince who had come to the stream to drink. Attracted by the perfume of roses, he plucked up the leaf and, on opening it, was surprised to find a strand of silken hair.

When the prince came home, his father saw at once that

he was ill, so pale and downcast did he look. 'What ails you, my son?' his father asked.

Showing him the scented lock of hair, the young prince said, 'Sire, I have fallen in love with the owner of this strand of hair. I fear I shall die unless I find its mistress and wed her.'

So the king sent heralds throughout the realm to find the maiden with rose-scented hair that shone like burnished ebony. And in the passing of time Dorani came to hear about the royal mission; she told her father wistfully, 'If it is the prince's wish to marry me, so be it, but tell him this: I will be his bride only if he lets me spend each night alone.'

The perfume seller went gladly to the palace and, on being shown before the king, told him of his daughter's wish. The king considered the condition strange, but eventually agreed, since his son was so ill.

All was soon arranged and the wedding took place amid the usual celebrations. At first, the prince was so happy just to have Dorani by him that he said nothing of the unusual pact. Yet as the days went by his joy turned to despair. For his wife sat silent all through the day, her head buried in her hands. She would not utter a single word. And at night she vanished, as if swallowed up by the dusky gloom.

One afternoon, as the prince was wandering in the palace grounds, he came upon the royal gardener; the old man had served long years and had learnt all about the power of herbs.

On asking of the flowers, the rains and the good soil, the prince then shared his burden with the loyal sage, 'How miserable I am, old friend, that I have wed a wife as radiant as the stars, yet cannot win her love. She sits sad and silent all through the day just like a marble statue; she utters not a sound, nor will she gaze at me. At night she disappears I know not where.'

The old man handed the prince some powder ground from the roots of certain herbs. 'Tonight, when your wife is about to leave you,' said the sage, 'sprinkle this powder upon your head and you will be invisible. Then you can follow her wherever she goes and thus unlock the mystery.'

The prince thanked the man and concealed the powder in his turban.

That night, as Dorani went to leave the palace, the prince quickly sprinkled the magic powder on his head and hurried after his lovely bride. Just as the old man had said, he was unseen by all as he followed his wife into the streets and through the town. Heavily veiled, she wandered down unfamiliar lanes until she came to a lofty mansion.

At the gates she removed one veil; and then, as she reached the entrance hall, she removed another veil. She climbed some stairs and at a door she unveiled for the third time, thus revealing her lovely face. Once inside the room she sat down before two bowls: one full of rose petals, one of milk. Maidservants rubbed and washed her with petals dipped in milk, then brought her sweetmeats to eat and sherbet to slake her thirst.

They dressed her in a shimmering sari, wound strings of pearls about her neck, bangles and beads around her arms and ankles, then crowned her shining hair with roses. Her watching husband had never seen her look so lovely.

When she was dressed, she sat down on a stool within a

canopy of silken curtains, out of the prince's sight. At that moment, Indira the Fairy Queen appeared and sat cross-legged upon a velvet throne; before her lay a magic lute that, at a signal from the Queen, began to play the most bewitching music.

The moment the lilting notes rang out, Dorani lifted up her voice to sing so sweetly that lute and voice blended as one. Since the prince had never heard her speak, nor seen her part her lips in song, he greatly wondered at the sound. And moving one curtain slightly, he watched entranced as Dorani sang throughout the night.

Just before the dawn, Indira gave a signal for the lute to stop, and Dorani ceased her song. Then the queen asked sternly, 'Why was the curtain drawn aside tonight? Did you tell your husband anything?'

Dorani vowed she had not breathed a word. Perhaps she had failed to draw the curtains tightly. She would certainly make sure she did the following night. With that she retraced her steps to her husband's home, donning the three veils on the way. The prince meanwhile walked invisible behind her and only took his normal form when safely inside the palace walls. And there he found Dorani, sad and silent, her head buried in her hands.

For a while the prince said nothing, then presently he spoke, 'I dreamed a most peculiar dream last night, Dorani.'

And he described in detail all that had happened.

Dorani seemed not to heed his words, yet when he came to praise her singing, she looked up with a start. His voice was trembling and his eyes were shining as he tried to paint a picture of her song.

'Was it really a dream?' she wondered. 'How could he know all that passed last night? Why does he single out my song?'

Only that one time did she glance up; then, as usual, she kept her head bowed the whole day through. As night descended, she left once more with the unseen prince close by. All went as it had the night before: the veils and bowls, the saris and the pearls. But this time she sang even more sweetly than the night before. In the morning the prince told his wife of what he'd seen, enfolding it all within a dream.

Once he had finished, she looked at him and softly asked, 'Tell me, O prince, was it a dream? Or were you really there?'

The prince loved his wife and could not lie. 'I followed you,' he sighed.

'But why?' she asked.

'It is quite simple,' the prince declared. 'I love you very much.'

Dorani blushed and said no more. She sat silent the rest of the day. However, just before dusk as she rose to go, she told the prince, 'If truly you love me as you say, then remain here tonight; that will test your love.'

The prince did precisely as she had asked.

That night Dorani sang so well that by dawn the Fairy Queen was even more enthralled and offered the maid any gift her heart desired.

At first she was silent, but when asked again, she quietly

replied, 'Give me the magic lute.'

Indira was cross with herself for being so rash; but a promise had to be kept. So she thrust the lute into Dorani's hands. 'You will not come here again,' she gruffly said, 'since no other gift I may offer will enchant you as much. Take the lute and be free.'

In silence Dorani bore her gift away, never to return. When she came home she at once asked the prince what dreams he had had the night before. He smiled with joy: for of her own free will, she had spoken to him first.

'No dreams have I had in the night just passed, though a dream appears to me now. Not of what was, but is to come, what might be now that you are free.'

Throughout that day Dorani sat quietly by, though she talked softly when spoken to and she looked up at the prince now and then. As evening fell and the hour drew on, the time came for her to go. Yet she lingered on and made no move to leave.

With hope in his eyes, the prince dared to ask, 'Will you stay with me tonight?'

At that she rose and ran to his arms, kissing him and holding him close. 'Yes, yes, my lord. Never again will I leave your side.'

Thus the prince won his bride from the Fairy Queen, for human love proved stronger than the fairy's spell.

Sleeping Beauty

Once upon a time there was a queen who had no child. Time passed and, when all hope was lost, she gave birth at last to a lovely daughter. How happy were the queen and her husband King Florestan. A grand christening was proclaimed. To it were invited many lords and ladies, and the six fairies of the realm – to act as fairy godmothers.

And they called the baby princess, Aurora.

The christening was followed by a ball. As the guests arrived, each one was announced by the Lord Chamberlain Cantalabutte and four trumpeters. In one corner of the royal ballroom, on a dais, stood the golden cradle of the infant princess, watched over by her loyal nursemaids. Even the trumpet fanfare that greeted the arrival of each fairy did not disturb her slumbers.

First to arrive was Candide, Fairy of the Crystal Fountain, all dressed in robes of glittering white. She curtseyed low before the king and queen, then placed a gift – a garland of pale water lilies – beside the royal cradle.

Next came Fleur, Fairy of the Enchanted Meadow, wearing a flowing gown with all the wild flowers embroidered on it. She presented a bouquet of fragrant flowers, and laid it beside the water lilies.

Then came Violante, Fairy of the Woodland Glade, all clad in browns and greens, with a gift of woodland blossoms to lay before the princess.

After her came Canarie, Fairy of the Song Birds, dressed in dove greys and peacock blues. Her present was a sweetly-singing yellow canary in a gilded cage.

The fifth fairy, Mignonne, Fairy of the Golden Vine, was attired in robes of shining gold; she placed before the cradle a basket of fruits from the fields and orchards – grapes and peaches, pears and plums.

As the final fanfare sounded, all heads turned to see the loveliest fairy of all. The guests could guess at once from her dress that it was the dainty Lilac Fairy. After a low curtsey to the royal pair, she lifted her magic wand, about to pronounce her wish for the sleeping child. But just at that moment a clap of thunder echoed through the ballroom and a flash of lightning startled all the assembled throng.

It woke up the Princess Aurora and made her cry.

The doors of the ballroom burst open and a frightened page scurried in to tell the king, 'Your majesty! The wicked Fairy Carabosse is coming in her carriage. And she is in a raging temper, that is plain.'

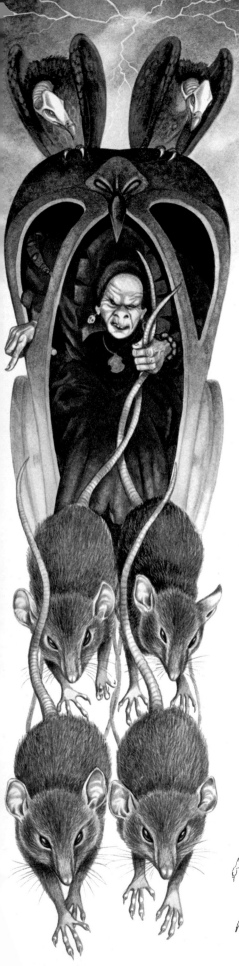

Straightaway the Lord Chamberlain clasped his head in his hands. 'Pray pardon me, sire,' he cried. 'It's all my fault: no one had seen Carabosse for full fifty years and I had cast her out of mind. I sent her no invitation to the christening.'

As the Chamberlain stood there trembling, the doors flew open once again and in rushed a carriage pulled by four grey rats and with vultures perching on the top. The carriage halted before the royal throne and an ancient crone in dark red robes stepped out.

It was the wicked Fairy Carabosse.

She marched straight up to Princess Aurora and, shaking a bony finger over the golden cradle, she put a curse upon the new-born babe.

'Death shall come to you, Aurora,' she said. 'Before you are full grown you shall prick your finger on a spindle and you shall die. Let that be punishment for ignoring Fairy Carabosse!'

The assembled company was overwhelmed. The queen fainted clean away, the king looked on in helpless desolation, the lords and ladies gasped in horror, the loyal nursemaids wept and sobbed. In the meantime, the wicked Fairy Carabosse gave an evil cackle, stepped into her carriage and drove unchallenged from the palace amid rumblings of mocking thunder.

And then, above the thunder, came the calm voice of the Lilac Fairy, 'Fear not, your majesties. I have yet to make my gift.'

Everyone turned to listen to the Fairy's words. The nursemaids dried their tears, the queen was roused out of her swoon, the king looked on in expectation.

''Tis true I can't undo what's said to come. Yet I can touch her with the thorn of sleep, so that when she pricks her finger she will slumber on until a prince is found with courage and pure heart to right the wrong and wake her with a kiss.'

On hearing this joyful news, the lords and ladies danced around the ballroom, while the king and queen and all the fairy godmothers gathered by the golden cradle. At once the king issued a proclamation:

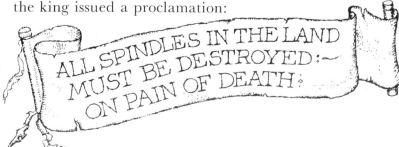

ALL SPINDLES IN THE LAND MUST BE DESTROYED:~ ON PAIN OF DEATH:

By the time the proclamation was written, Princess Aurora was once again in peaceful slumber.

Time passed.

Princess Aurora grew up and became more beautiful with each passing year. Wherever she went a whole crowd of loyal nursemaids followed in her wake, eager to protect her should a spindle find its way, undetected, into the royal household.

On her sixteenth birthday, when the Princess came of age, a grand birthday party was held in her honour. Guests were invited from all over the kingdom and beyond: lord and lady, country maid and tiller of the fields, even four foreign princes who came as suitors – one from England, one from Poland, one from Italy and one from India. Each prince danced with the princess in turn and each presented her with a different coloured rose.

In the midst of this rejoicing, as the princess mingled with the crowd, she felt a hand clutch at her arm. On looking round she saw an ancient woman in dark red robes, leaning on a wooden stick, her face concealed behind a flowing hood. In one hand, she held a bouquet of red roses which she held out to the princess.

'This is my birthday present to you, dearie,' the old crone said, giving her the flowers.

The princess was delighted. As she looked up to thank her, the strange figure in the dark red robes had vanished – as if she'd never been.

The birthday princess ran excitedly across the palace lawn to show the bouquet to her parents. She held it tight lest it slip from her hands in her happy flight. But just as she reached the king and queen, she pricked her finger on a thorn and a red spot of blood appeared. Mindful of her parents' warning about the spell cast upon her as a child, Princess Aurora grew pale and frightened.

But nothing happened and she realized that thorns could do no harm. To reassure herself, she began to pluck roses from the bouquet, offering them to her father, mother and her suitors. In so doing she uncovered a spindle hidden in the middle of the roses and flung it quickly to the ground.

It was too late.

She felt a piercing pain throughout her body, her head whirled and she fainted at her father's feet.

King Florestan quickly put his arms about her shoulders

to lift her from the ground, but she could not be roused. As he looked up in despair, he caught a glimpse of that strange red-robed figure watching from behind a distant tree. Her hood was now flung back and she was laughing shrilly.

At once he recognized the evil face of Carabosse.

Doctors were summoned immediately, and they came fussing and bustling to try their cures: they rubbed Aurora's temples with rosewater and tickled the souls of her feet. All to no avail.

Knowing in his heart that the wicked Fairy's curse had taken hold, King Florestan had his daughter's body carried by the four princes to the finest chamber of the palace and gently placed upon a velvet couch.

Princess Aurora slept on soundly. She neither ate nor drank, nor did her form or colour fade. Her cheeks were flushed like pink carnations, her lips remained a ruby rose colour. And though her eyes were closed, folk knew she was not dead by the rising of her breast as she softly breathed.

So lovely did she look that all who saw her called her Sleeping Beauty.

Now at the time this accident occurred, the Lilac Fairy was in the realm of Matakin twelve thousand leagues away. The sad news reached her on the north-east wind. In haste she rode through the sky in her red chariot of fire until she reached the grief-filled palace.

'There is nothing I can do to break the spell,' she told the king and queen. 'However, though my magic cannot reach

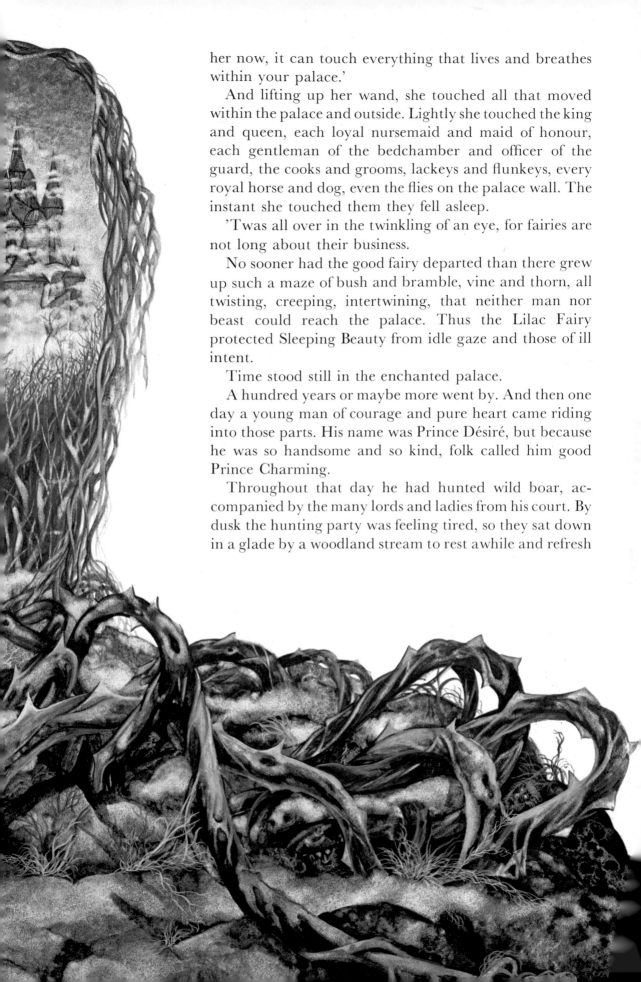

her now, it can touch everything that lives and breathes within your palace.'

And lifting up her wand, she touched all that moved within the palace and outside. Lightly she touched the king and queen, each loyal nursemaid and maid of honour, each gentleman of the bedchamber and officer of the guard, the cooks and grooms, lackeys and flunkeys, every royal horse and dog, even the flies on the palace wall. The instant she touched them they fell asleep.

'Twas all over in the twinkling of an eye, for fairies are not long about their business.

No sooner had the good fairy departed than there grew up such a maze of bush and bramble, vine and thorn, all twisting, creeping, intertwining, that neither man nor beast could reach the palace. Thus the Lilac Fairy protected Sleeping Beauty from idle gaze and those of ill intent.

Time stood still in the enchanted palace.

A hundred years or maybe more went by. And then one day a young man of courage and pure heart came riding into those parts. His name was Prince Désiré, but because he was so handsome and so kind, folk called him good Prince Charming.

Throughout that day he had hunted wild boar, accompanied by the many lords and ladies from his court. By dusk the hunting party was feeling tired, so they sat down in a glade by a woodland stream to rest awhile and refresh

themselves. The prince was somehow rather sad: a cloud of
dark depression hung over him for no apparent reason.
When his comrades sighted a wild boar and rushed off in
pursuit, the prince remained alone, sitting by the woodland stream.

It grew dark, the bright Moon peeped from behind a
cloud and cast a purple glow upon the water. All of a
sudden, a strange boat appeared, gliding up the stream. It
was being drawn by three giant butterflies attached by
silken threads, and as it reached the water's edge where the
prince was sitting, a graceful maiden stepped out all
dressed in lilac lace.

It was the Lilac Fairy.

'Good-day, Prince Désiré,' she said by way of greeting.
'I have come to lift the cloud of gloom that hangs above
your brow and take you on a journey to save a dear
princess.'

And she told him the story of Sleeping Beauty.

To illustrate the tale she told, she waved her wand and
in the clouds above their heads there appeared a vision of
the fair Aurora sleeping on her couch within the enchanted
palace.

'How beautiful she is,' sighed the prince. 'Pray, tell me
how I can save her.'

The Lilac Fairy took the prince into her boat and
together they sailed throughout the night across the realm.

Finally the boat came to rest before a dense, dark forest.

'This is the forest,' said the Lilac Fairy, 'in which stands the palace of the Princess Aurora and all the royal court of King Florestan.'

The prince gazed in dismay at the tangled bush of thorn and bramble that blocked their path. For sure, no mortal being could find a way through.

'Follow me,' the Lilac Fairy said, taking him by the hand. 'I know a secret path that opens to my magic wand.'

She led him forward up the bank and, to his surprise, a path opened up before them. The bush and bramble parted, the vines and creepers untwined their gnarled fingers to let them pass. After some time they came to a flight of moss-covered steps that led up to the gates of what had once been a splendid palace.

Passing through the gates, the prince moved down an avenue lined with human statues and through the palace courtyard until he came to open doors. He walked in past the sleeping guards, brushing aside the cobwebs and dangling creepers, and began to climb the marble stairs. The air was cold and damp, the light was dim, for no sunbeams pierced the ivy-covered windows.

At the top of the staircase, the prince moved on past sleeping footmen and silent chambermaids until he came to the room in which the velvet couch was standing. Then he and the Lilac Fairy stood before the sleeping maid.

The prince's heart overflowed with love as he gazed upon the lovely girl. Never in his life had he set eyes on such tender beauty. He could not help but fall in love at first fond sight.

'How lovely she looks in gentle sleep,' he murmured softly. Bending down, he planted a gentle kiss upon her brow.

The princess awoke.

She stared uncertainly at this intruder on her dreams; and then slowly her gaze mellowed into purest love.

Presently, all the palace was awake, stirring, stretching,

bustling busily about their chores. The king and queen smiled fondly on their daughter and gave instructions to the faithful Cantalabutte; the four foreign princes continued the conversation they had begun one hundred years before; the dogs barked, the cats miaowed, the birds twittered gaily in the trees.

The palace suddenly grew light and warm: sunlight streamed in through doors and windows, making the dust and cobwebs fade right away. Outside, the dense forest faded and gave way to green lawns and rose beds, lakes and fountains – just as it all had been one hundred years before upon Aurora's birthday.

Supper was served and violins played romantic melodies. Truth to tell, Prince Charming was a little surprised, though he did not remark on it. For the tunes were so old-fashioned and the ladies' gowns were like those his grandmother used to wear.

After supper, without more ado, the young pair were led to the palace chapel and were married. Their wedding was followed by celebrations to which all the world was invited. The six fairy godmothers were there, and so were all the favourite characters of fairyland. Each came to dance and pay their compliments to the happy pair.

All the merry company joined the dance. Puss in Boots danced with Jack his master; Bluebeard danced with his first wife; Red Riding Hood danced with the Big Bad Wolf; Cinderella danced with her handsome prince; Beauty danced with Beast; Goldilocks danced with all three bears at once; and, funniest of all, the Giant tried to dance with wee Tom Thumb.

In short, a good time was had by all.

The wicked Fairy Carabosse was quite forgotten. She had never been seen again in all those years. Some said she had been deafened by her own thunder and blinded by her lightning. But if it were true, it served her right.

The hour soon came for Prince Charming and Princess Aurora to set off on their honeymoon. Leading the way down to the stream, the Lilac Fairy helped them into her waiting boat. And with a wave of her magic wand, she sent the boat gliding smoothly down the stream, pulled as before on silken threads by the three giant butterflies. As the king and queen and all the guests waved goodbye, the Lilac Fairy smiled a contented smile.

For she knew that Good had conquered Evil once again.

Notes for the Reader

Children who are told fairy tales are cleverer, calmer, more open-minded and more balanced than those who are not – so concluded three German researchers (H.G. Wahn, W. Hesse, U. Schaefer in *Suddeutsche Zeitung*, 24 June 1980). They found, further, that imagination, vocabulary, memory and manner of speech improved in proportion to the aural and visual impressions the child received from fairy tales. Therefore, in the modern world of competing images from television, comics and picture books, fairy tales play an essential part in education. They have, of course, lasted down the ages simply because they are the best stories in the world.

But not if they are told any old how.

There are plenty of collections of fairy tales in which eye-catching pictures take precedence over words. Yet words have the most important role in a story. There is a world of difference between a robust, direct and witty translation of Charles Perrault, Hans Andersen, or Jakob and Wilhelm Grimm, and the sugar-sweet versions to be found in many fairy-tale books. Translating fairy tales – whether written by Ibsen, Andersen or Collodi – should be no different from translating the works of any eminent author.

That is why in this book I have, wherever possible, translated and consulted original materials, as in the case of the four great European folk sources: Perrault of France, Andersen of Denmark, the Grimms of Germany, and Alexander Afanasiev of Russia. I have also dipped into the treasures of Scotland's Robert Chambers, England's Joseph Jacobs, Holland's Tjaard W.R. de Haan, Czechoslovakia's Bozena Nemcova and of the Irish-American Jeremiah Curtin. Three sources included – Italy's Carlo Collodi, Norway's Henrik Ibsen and Senegal's René Guillot – are authors in their own right beyond the fairy tale. But they, like the Urals storyteller Pavel Bazhov, provide a rich vein to mine in this most enduring form of children's literature.

In selecting tales for inclusion, I have cast the net wide so as to take in different cultures for the benefit of our own modern multi-ethnic communities. And in an age when so many sexual stereotypes are being challenged, I have tried to strike a balance between stories featuring men and women as the heroes. Finally, this is a book jointly conceived and worked upon by a team of colleagues: artists, editors, designer and myself, thus hopefully producing an integral whole.

For the benefit of students of fairy tale, I provide below a few notes on source references.

The Rainbow and the Bread Fruit Flower. This is an Australian Aborigine story kindly sent to me by the Australian writer Alan Marshall, and published in his *People of the Dreamtime* (Melbourne, 1952). I have changed the text somewhat to blend with the style of this book. *The Twelve Months*. This is my translation of the Bohemian fairy tale collected by the major Czechoslovak folklorist Božena Němcova and published in her *Zlata Kniha Pohadek* (*Golden Book of Fairy Tales*), Prague 1973.

The Black Bull of Norroway. This old Scottish fairy tale is adapted from Robert Chambers *Popular Rhymes of Scotland*, published in

Edinburgh in 1870. The story has many versions, with the bull sometimes red, white, brown or black. The 'washerwife', 'hen-wife' or 'spey-wife' is usually a helpful fortune-teller; and the 'bake me a bannock (oatmeal cake) and roast me a collop' (portion [of meat]) is a common device in Scottish stories.

The Blue Baba of the Marsh. This tale from the Ural Mountains is from a collection by the Russian ex-miner Pavel Bazhov (1879–1950) who learned the folk history of the Urals while working in the copper mines and goldfields. I have translated the story (*Sinyushkin kolodets*) from *Malakhitovaya shkatulka* (*The Malachite Box*) published in Sverdlovsk in 1959 (the year in which I first heard it while recovering from my first bout of Russian hospitality in a Sverdlovsk hotel bed).

The Fairies of the Evening Star. This Cree Indian myth was gathered at the end of the last century by Margaret Bemister of Canada and published in *Thirty Indian Legends of Canada* (Macmillan, 1917).

Kaatje's Treasure. This popular Dutch story of hope for dreamers comes from the Haarlem area of northern Netherlands and was kindly translated for me by Jon Willis from *Nederlandse Volks Sprookjes* by Dr. Tjaard W.R. de Haan (Utrecht, 1966); its original title is 'De schat in de bedstee'.

Rapunzel. The well-known story is translated from the *Kinder und Hausmärchen* of Jakob and Wilhelm Grimm, published in Germany in 1812. The 'Rapunzel', incidentally, is rampion, a herb whose leaves are used in salads, and whose white root is eaten raw like radish.

Tovik Tomte and the Trolls. This popular Swedish fairy story, written down by Alfred Smedberg on the well-loved theme of the gentle little tomtes against the wicked shaggy trolls, is taken from *Bland tomtar och troll* (Among Tomtes and Trolls) by Cyrus Granér. I have slightly altered names (Tjovik to Tovik, Tjarfa to Tarfa) to facilitate pronunciation.

The Tinder Box. This is a fairly literal translation of Hans Andersen's story, written in 1835 when the author was 29 and short of money; hence the tale's appeal to him.

Lotus Blossom. This is a Tibetan story which I have taken from a Russian translation of the original Tibetan: *Kamenny Lev. Tibetskie narodnye shazki* (*The Stone Lion. Tibetan Fairy Tales*) by Yuri Parfionovich, Moscow, 1976. In the original story 'The Girl and the Demon Brothers', the heroine's name is 'Paradise Flower'.

The Frog Princess. This Russian fairy tale is well known to many from the Grimm story *The Frog Prince.* The strong matriarchal influence on Russian folk takes is here evident in this reversal of the roles. I have translated the tale 'Tsarevna Lyagushka' from *Narodnye russkie skazki* (*Russian Folk Tales*) by Alexander Afanasiev, published in 1855.

Pinocchio. I have abridged this well-known tale from Carlo Collodi's novel about the little wooden puppet, first published in Italy in 1882.

The Princess and the Peas. This story is taken directly from Andersen.

The Little Mermaid. This is an abridged version of Hans Christian Andersen's own favourite fairy tale. As with all his tales it is modelled on the folk tradition rather than adapted from it. I have translated this and subsequent Andersen stories from the Danish.

Jack and the Beanstalk. I have adapted this rumbustious old English tale from the version recorded by Joseph Jacobs (which he heard in Australia in 1860) in his *English Fairy Tales* (London, 1890).

Children of the Wind. This extremely beautiful African story comes from *Nouveaux Contes d'Afrique* (*New Tales from Africa*), written by René Guillot and collected mainly in Senegal.

The Fisherman of Kinsale. There are several Irish and Scottish Gaelic versions of this engaging story (see Campbell's *Popular Tales of the West Highlands*, and Jacob's *Celtic Fairy Tales*). I have taken this version from *Irish Folk Tales* (Dublin, 1944), collected by the Irish-American folklorist Jeremiah Curtin in the last century. He took down the story in Gaelic from the blind storyteller Diarmaid Ó Dubháin. Diarmaid was evidently bemused that someone should actually keep him in ale for simply 'telling lying stories to the gentleman from morn til night.'

Tom Thumb in Deventer. This somewhat unusual episode in the adventures of the little lad is set in the north of the Netherlands on the River Ijssel. I have had to 'protect' tender eyes and ears (not to say 'noses') from some of the original Dutch ribaldry. . . . The story 'Wat Klein Duimpje in Deventer overkam' was kindly translated for me by Jon Willis from *Nederlandse Volks Sprookjes.*

The Snow Queen. This is an abridged version of Andersen's famous fairy tale, translated from the Danish.

The Little White Duck. This has been translated for me from Spanish by my friend and colleague José Amodia.

The Golden Goose. This well-known funny story is translated from the Grimm collection.

The Aztec Sun is based on a number of Aztec stories about the origin of the Sun and the world's creation; some of these may be found in *Stories Told by the Aztecs Before the Spaniards*

Came by Carleton Beals (Abelard-Schuman, London, 1970).

Peer Gynt is a popular 'wandering' character in Norwegian folklore who features widely in the collected folk tales of Asbjörnsen and Moe. The story here is adapted from the play by Henrik Ibsen on which Grieg's famous Peer Gynt Suites were based.

Dorani. This Indian story is adapted from Andrew Lang's *Olive Fairy Book.* I have restored some of the original Indian characteristics to the text after consultation with an Asian colleague at Bradford Children's Library.

Sleeping Beauty. This is the first story in the Perrault collection *Histoires ou contes du temps passé*, published in Paris in 1697. It was known as 'La Belle au Bois Dormant' (The Beauty in the Sleeping Wood). I have adapted the French version to Marius Petipa's libretto for Tchaikovsky's ballet.